For Alvie.

Author's Note

This novel began several years ago with an attempt at flash fiction: one thousand words about a carnival worker falling in love with an opera singer in the 1950s. I knew even at the time that the characters had more story than I could include in a thousand words, so I set it aside, thinking that one day, when the time was right, I would come back to it. Like so many things in my "I'll come back to this idea when I'm ready" drawer, it slipped completely from my mind.

Then in 2014 my best friend, Rachel, sent me a "Call for Submissions" from a small press that I did not yet have on my radar: Interlude Press was seeking stories of "Summer Love." I was excited about the anthology's concept and after brainstorming decided there was nothing else on this earth that screamed summer to me, having grown up in my small, festival-obsessed hometown, than a carnival. From there, I wrote the short story, "The Fire-Eater's Daughter," published in the *Summer Love* anthology, which tells the tale of Ruth and Constance.

Immensely pleased with the people I was lucky enough to work with on *Summer Love,* I knew I wanted to work with them again on a full length novel and that I wanted to continue working in the world of "The Fire-Eater's Daughter." I outlined and outlined, but then I remembered the flash fiction piece, also about a carnival, languishing away in my "I'll come back to this" drawer. I rescued the story and began to flesh it out with historical research and new details, slowly expanding it into the story you are about to read.

Chapter One

~Cleveland, Ohio. 1957. Late July.~

That time, just after sunset, when the lights inside blocked out the darkened streets and turned the diner into a cocoon, that was Abby's favorite time. She felt safe, locked away, as if all the trouble in the world had to be left outside. Outside were her vocal instructor's angry pronouncements that she would never get anywhere in the opera world unless she improved her Italian, followed by Abby's insistences that she had grown up speaking Italian, so her pronunciation should be fine, thank you very much. Outside were the stuck-up girls in the chorus who told her she would never be a real singer because she was far too ugly. Outside were her nonna's encroaching senility, her four younger siblings, and her father, who spent all his time either working at the steelyards or sleeping. The diner, however, was a cozy island in the vast sea of Cleveland at night.

Of course, the world inside the diner had its own fair share of troubles: unreasonable customers, tip-stiffers, Sal getting it into his head to make the plates look gourmet so wait times skyrocketed. Most of the time, though, its challenges were simpler than those of the outer world. Inside things, Abby could handle.

She hummed along to the jukebox as she wiped up a strawberry milkshake spill and tried to ignore the oblivious couple responsible for it. Their fingers interlaced as they walked out of the diner with hands locked just as their eyes were. Neither seemed to have noticed their waitress. As far as Abby was concerned, that was just as well.

Being so close to the Cedar Lee Theatre, the diner was a popular date spot, serving an overwhelming share of Coventry neighborhood couples each Friday night. Abby wasn't jealous. Sal and Roman, the cooks, heckled her from time to time about being a single girl in a land full of couples, but it only really bothered her when they brought it up. When her friends came in with their boy or girl du jour, she might feel a twinge of loneliness, but it never lasted long. Abby kept herself too busy working and saving for her opera classes to worry about dating anymore, at least since her last boyfriend had cheated on her twice.

"Abigail!" Roman called from the kitchen with a mischievous ring in his voice.

"It's just Abby," she replied, turning around and taking the basket of fries he had just set in the pass-through window.

"Your favorite song's on the jukebox."

Abby stared at him, her nose wrinkled, somewhat puzzled until she heard Rosemary Clooney's fake Italian accent begin to drift through the diner. Noting the expectant smile on Roman's face, Abby rolled her eyes, then casually put down the fries and threw a towel at the jukebox. "You wanna be-a me, ah?" she mocked.

Roman and Sal laughed. She knew they had convinced someone to put the song on because they liked to see her reactions to it, but Abby didn't mind. She liked it when they laughed, even if it was at her. Theirs were hearty, thick, genuine laughs. So many customers laughed insincerely, as if trying to impress her or assuage their own guilt over paltry tips.

Shaking her head, she picked up the fries again. "You know I only do that for you."

"We love you, Abby!" both cooks chorused as one.

Once again, she rolled her eyes. Then she stepped away to deliver the fries.

As she made her way out from behind the counter, a hand took her by the elbow. Abby spun around to see Frank Butler, Coventry neighborhood's own Mr. Tall, Dark, and Handsome, and her very-ex-boyfriend. Practically every girl from Euclid to Shaker Heights had wanted him, but Abby had claimed him. Much to her later dismay. "Abigail Amaro," he trilled.

"It's just Abby." She jerked her elbow forward, trying to wrench it from Frank's grasp, but he held tight.

"My apologies, Abby Amaro. Fancy seeing you here."

"I work here, Frank; you know that." Still trying not to spill the tray of food, she jerked her elbow again. "Speaking of which, can you let go? Table six needs their fries."

"Table six can wait. I've got a question for you."

Abby took a deep breath, then stepped hard on Frank's foot. He let go of her elbow. She hurried to deliver the fries and get back behind the counter before Frank could cause any further trouble.

Too late.

The second she stepped behind the counter, she saw Frank seated at the end, waiting with an expectant grin plastered on his face and flanked by two other young men with muscular builds. Abby bit her lip; her job as a waitress was to ask for their order, but she didn't want to speak to them. She glanced at the pass-through window. Sal had his eye on her, as if waiting for confirmation that she wanted him to take care of it. She shook her head. As much as she wanted to dive into the kitchen and hide there for the rest of the night, she wasn't willing to actually do it. At least here, in the diner, there would be plenty of witnesses. Again she took a deep breath and steeled herself for the approach.

"What can I get for you?" she asked, not looking up from her notepad.

"Three chocolate malts," Frank said, keeping his voice low and smooth. "And three burgers. With pickles."

"Right." Abby nodded, slipped her pen behind her ear, and turned to go.

"One more thing, Miss Amaro."

Abby hated the way Frank said her name. His singsongy voice made it sound more like a schoolyard taunt than a name. "And that is?"

Frank dropped his voice to a pleading whisper. "Abby, look at me. This is kinda serious, and you know I don't do serious well."

"That's an understatement," Abby muttered.

"That's fair." Frank looked at each of his pseudo-bodyguards, then back at Abby. "I haven't always been great or faithful, I admit, but … things are starting to look up for me."

"Congratulations, Frank."

"No, I mean, I'm moving up in the world. In the next few years, I just know things are going to take off, and I think I want a good strong girl by my side when they do."

Abby stared, unsure how to process what he meant.

"Will you marry me, Abby?"

Abby couldn't speak. She couldn't move. She simply stared, unblinking. "What?"

Frank reached across the counter to take her hands, but she pulled them back. "Will you marry me?" he repeated.

The whole diner seemed to have gone still. Even though Frank had spoken quietly, Abby felt as if every eye were turned to look at her. Her stomach lurched. She wanted to ask a million questions, respond with a million no's, but the only word that came out of her mouth was a very small "Why?"

The smirk once again dancing on his lips, Frank leaned back in his chair a little as though examining her. "I say, Abby, do you think you're not worthy of me?"

Indignation rose in her throat. “No. Why on earth would I want to marry you?” She untied her apron and started into the kitchen, where Sal and Roman were both trying to pretend that they had not been listening and doing an incredibly poor job of it.

“C-can one of you get me a glass of water?” she asked, leaning against the back door, trying to catch a bit of the nighttime breeze.

Sal nodded. “On it.”

Roman wrapped her in a bear hug. Her tension melted away into the hug, and she was grateful for it. “When’s Natale coming?” he asked in a barely audible whisper.

Abby shook her head against Roman’s shoulder. She didn’t know.

“You want to give him a call? I can ask Marjorie to cover for you until close. She’ll understand.”

Sal held out a glass of water, and Abby drank it down in two gulps. “I can’t,” she said. “I should be able to handle this. He’s nothing to me.”

“He did a number on you, Abby. It takes a while to come back from something like that.”

The floor became unstable, but Abby refused to acknowledge it. She took a deep breath, closed her eyes, and then nodded slowly.

THE SILENCE IN NATALE’S CAR was deafening. He didn’t say a word when he picked her up, but Abby could see from the look on his face that he was worried. That look had appeared many a time since the two of them were children. Whenever something troubling happened, Natale’s eyes would take on a glassy, faraway quality, as if whatever he was seeing was miles down the road, and his lips would press together so tightly it would have taken a crowbar to pry them apart. Guilt roiled in Abby’s stomach; she knew that this time the look was because of her.

“Nate,” she whispered, only daring to break the silence in the quietest voice she could muster. “I’m fine, you know.”

Natale nodded, but did not say a word.

"Frank just rattled me a little. You know how he can be." Not wanting to press the matter, she let silence fall; but then Natale spoke.

"Yeah, I know exactly how Frank Butler can be, Abby. That's why I told you not to go steady with him in the first place." His tone had an authoritative edge that Abby didn't like, though she agreed with him.

"You're my brother, Nate, not my father."

They sighed dramatically, almost at the same time.

"What did he do, Abby? Did he threaten you? 'Cause I swear, if he did—"

"Nothing like that." Abby shook her head and glanced out the car window at the lights of the city rushing by. "He was just trying to rattle me. Told me he was coming up in the world and that he wanted me to marry him."

Natale stayed very quiet, but Abby could feel his eyes upon her. "And what did you say?" he finally asked, as he pulled the car to a stop on the street in front of their house.

"No! Of course," Abby said. "Look, Nate, he may have blinded me before, but I see Frank for what he is now: a rat."

"Good." Natale sighed. Abby knew her brother well enough to sense that the sigh was equal parts relief and concern. "Just be careful, okay? He may be a rat, but he's a pretty dangerous one."

The house was dark when Abby and Natale went inside. Natale kissed her cheek and departed for his room. As she made her way down the hall to the room she shared with her two younger sisters, Carla and Annette, Abby noticed a light coming from under one of the other doors: the one belonging to Nonna Gaetana.

Abby knocked lightly on the door, hoping that her grandmother had simply forgotten to turn off the light.

"*Cui?*" a woman's voice called out, sounding chipper despite the hour.

"*É* Abby, Nonna."

There was a pause, and then a joyous voice responded, "*Entra! Entra!*"

Abby slipped inside. Seated at her writing desk was Abby's grandmother—her father's mother—a petite older woman of about seventy. Her hair was still thick, but had turned from black to gray thanks to years of raising seven children and then assisting with six grandchildren. Her smile, though, had not been dimmed by time. "Abigaille," she cooed, holding out her hands. Abby crossed the room and took them.

"What are you doing up, Nonna?" she asked in her grandmother's native Sicilian dialect. Nonna Gaetana spoke English well enough, but she did not prefer it and, with age, she found it much easier to use the language she'd learned in childhood. She had pressed Abby to learn it as well, and, now that Nonna slipped into it so often, Abby was grateful that she had.

She squeezed Abby's hand, then let go, gesturing toward the papers and photographs laid out on the table. "I was writing to my family back home. I miss them."

Abby tried not to frown at the pictures. So many of the people in them were dead and gone now, but Abby had no way of knowing which, so she nodded. "I'm sure they miss you too."

With great care, Nonna Gaetana folded the paper in front of her and slipped it into an envelope, which she set off to the side. "But how is my Abigaille today?"

"Wonderful, Nonna," Abby said, sitting down on her grandmother's bed. During earlier days, she would have told her grandmother about everything from the spilled milkshake to Frank Butler's proposal, but now she didn't know if she could. There was a distance between them that Abby didn't know how to cross.

Nonna Gaetana beamed. "And your vocal classes? Am I going to see you in an opera soon?"

Abby didn't want to lie. Her classes weren't going particularly well, and the closest she would get to a role was somewhere in the back of the chorus. About to confess her frustration, she took a breath, but when she looked at the hopeful expression on her grandmother's face, she didn't think she could tell the truth either. "Any season now, Nonna," she said. "My coach has me working on an aria from *La sonnambula* right now."

"Ah, Bellini." Nonna Gaetana sighed. "He was Sicilian, you know."

"Yes, Nonna, you've mentioned that before."

"Don't you scoff at me, Abby. You have a gift and you have a duty to use it. When I was a little girl back home, we poor folk weren't even *allowed* in the opera houses. Now, my granddaughter will be one of the finest sopranos that this world has ever known."

Abby's face turned a fierce shade of scarlet. "Nonna …" She trailed off as her grandmother once again took her hands and held them tightly.

"My precious Abby. You are such a wonder. Promise me you will never give in to what the world expects from you. Live the life that you want to live and be strong and never ashamed. It took me too long to learn this, but promise me …"

Abby's eyes welled up with tears. Just a few weeks ago, her grandmother was pushing for her to get married, and to Frank of all people; this pronouncement was a complete reversal. What had caused the change? There was something final about her grandmother's words, and that terrified her. "Of course, Nonna. I promise."

Chapter Two

The next morning, Abby woke to a tugging on her arm. "Aaabbbyyy!" Annette's shrill five-year-old voice burst through any remnants of sleep Abby might have had left.

She reached with her free arm for a pillow to throw at her youngest sister, but came up empty-handed. She groaned. "Ugh, Annette, what do you want?"

"Natale promised we'd go the carnival today!"

Abby pulled the covers over her head to block out the light and, she hoped, Annette's voice. "Natale was mistaken."

"Pleeeaaase, Abby," the little girl begged, drawing out her syllables like a master manipulator. "It's the laaast day. And the flyer said there would be poonnniiiieees!"

"Good God!" Abby exclaimed in exasperation, throwing the covers off and climbing out of bed. There would be no sleeping now. She glared at her baby sister contemptuously. The little girl knew how to get what she wanted. "You," she began, shaking her head to clear the grogginess. It didn't work as well as she had hoped. "You have got a pair of lungs on you there, Annie. How about you put them to use and ask Natale to make your big sister some coffee?"

"And then the carnival?" Annette asked, her eyes large and hopeful.

"And then the carnival."

Annette let out a high-pitched squeal of joy and raced from the room. Abby shook her head. Natale was always so much better with the little ones, looking out for things that would make them happy. She hadn't known that a carnival was in town, let alone that her siblings would like to go. Of course she wanted them to be happy; she just couldn't read them as Natale did. Natale could read anyone. It was one of his more annoying qualities. She tried not to let that fact bother her yet again, but dressed quickly and hurried down to the kitchen where the coffee lived.

"Morning, sleepyhead," Natale chirped, holding out a mug of the precious liquid.

Abby slurped it down, then looked around at the assembled Amaro siblings: Leon, soon to be a newly minted teenager, slouched against the wall while the slightly younger Joseph attempted to imitate him; and Carla and Annette, the two youngest, sat at the corner of the table and watched Abby expectantly, perhaps assuming that if she didn't agree to the day's plan, only the boys would be allowed to go. "I hear we're going to a carnival today?"

Annette let out another happy little squeal.

Leon rolled his eyes. "This one has professional fighters," he pronounced with some relish. "Patrick Donovan at school says that sometimes they pick people out of the audience to fight them!"

Natale and Abby exchanged a glance; neither wanted to be the one to tell him he was probably too young for such a feat. They seemed to decide to cross that bridge when they came to it. "Well, that sounds like fun," Abby forced out.

"Is everybody ready?" Natale asked, voice still chipper. Was his tone masking something?

The group nodded assent.

"Then get to the car. Abby and I will be right out."

Ah. There it was. "Abby and I will be right out." The rest of the Amaro children ran out to Natale's car and waited.

Abby focused on her brother as he put a few of the breakfast dishes away. "Spit it out, Nate. What couldn't you say in front of them?"

Natale frowned and turned to face her. "There was a nasty note for you in the mailbox this morning."

Abby tried to sip the last of her coffee nonchalantly, hoping that the tension beginning to develop between her shoulders wouldn't show. "Was there?"

"Tell that …" Natale trailed off, obviously uncomfortable with whatever word came next. He shook his head as if the memory of it hurt. "Tell that … sister of yours, it's not like she can do better."

"Nate, Frank's just trying to rattle my cage. Ignore him."

"After what he did to you, Abby?"

"I'm over it. Some anonymous note's not gonna change that."

A car horn beeped out front, and Natale shook his head. "I worry that you're just covering up what you really feel."

"Let me worry about that, okay?"

Beep. This time Natale laughed. "We better get going, I guess."

Abby nodded. "What about Nonna?"

"She said she wanted to stay in today and work on her letters. Maybe listen to her stories on the radio, and I quote, 'Without constant interruptions.'"

"Maybe I should stay with her." She was still thinking about what Nonna had said the night before. Part of her hoped that one of their chats—like the ones they'd had when she was small—would sort out Nonna's meaning.

"No, Abby, come on. I need you. You're better with the girls."

"I don't know about that." She stood up from the table and rinsed her coffee mug. "Will you buy me an elephant ear?"

"You got it."

Plate of fried dough in hand, Abby and her siblings walked the midway. Though they wouldn't let them play any games, Abby and

Natale did buy each of their siblings a giant stick of cotton candy and two trips on a haunted house train ride that, both times, left Annette in tears and begging to go again.

"I still don't see why I can't try to ring the bell. I bet I could do it. I'm the strongest in my class. I can lift my desk," Leon persisted as Natale once again directed him away from the young tattooed man who was chanting, "Prove yourself a man!"

"I wanna try too!" Joseph said, crossing his arms and pouting.

"And me!" Annette chimed in, more gleefully than her brothers.

Natale looked at Abby in frustration, but she smirked back. "This was your idea," she mouthed.

Then, from behind them, they heard Carla scream. They spun, ready to rescue her from heaven knows what, and saw her pointing at a man with a face full of what appeared to be pins. Abby went to hush her, but Carla continued screaming and wouldn't lower her pointing arm. A few seconds later Annette and Joseph had joined her.

Abby tried herding them away, but the three children stayed rooted to the spot.

Then a thick, heavy voice that sounded like the villain in a bad science fiction movie spoke. "Pardon me. I'm sorry. I didn't see the little ones. I was just coming out for a smoke." It was the man wearing pins in his face. Fearful of how they might react, Abby watched her younger siblings.

"It's not your fault," Natale said, waving a hand. "They've had a little too much sugar."

"Perhaps they'd like to see the show?"

The looks on the younger Amaro siblings' faces turned from fear to eagerness.

"I don't know ..." Abby began, looking at the man. The kids could barely handle him, but to her he seemed tame.

"They see worse in movies," Natale said with a laugh.

The man nodded. "But we're better." He lifted a corner of the tent flap. "This way! If anyone gives you trouble on the other side, tell them Boleslaw is following."

Abby frowned as her brother led the rest of the family through. She had a vague sense of foreboding; in the back of her mind, a small voice whispered, "Don't go. It will change everything."

"Miss?" Boleslaw asked, gesturing toward the tent. She took a deep breath and went through.

What she saw inside the tent took her breath away. The bright light of day had dimmed to an almost insubstantial twilight. As her eyes adjusted, Abby could see that they had entered from the side, and, while they did not have a direct view of the slightly raised wooden platform, what she saw upon it was still exceptional: A dark-haired young woman in a shimmering white costume twirled a flaming hula hoop about her waist. Abby cast a sideways glance at her siblings. Carla's mouth had dropped open in utter awe.

The girl finished her act by throwing the hula hoop into the air. The audience gasped as if expecting the canvas tent to catch fire and burn them alive. Seeming to ignore their fear, the girl caught hold of the hoop and carefully slid her hand along it. The flames disappeared. The onlookers burst into thunderous applause as she bowed and hurried behind a curtain. Seconds later, she was replaced by a highly muscled man with a snake around his shoulders. Leon yelped.

Before their eyes, the snake began to wrap itself around the man's body, tighter and tighter, and his face turned redder and redder. Abby couldn't look away. "It's going to kill him," Joseph whispered to Annette, who clamped her hands over her mouth to keep from screaming. Natale shushed them.

The man dropped to the ground. Abby choked back her own scream. She immediately looked to Boleslaw, feeling stricken.

"Now, now, don't you worry for Gregor," Boleslaw hissed in her direction, seeming to take pity on her. Seconds later, the man stood up, snake once again draped loosely over his arms. The audience let out a collective sigh of relief before applauding.

Gregor walked to the edge of the stage and bowed as the applause continued. Then he squinted and appeared to examine the crowd as he passed up and down the length of the platform. "You!" he shouted, pointing into the audience. The dim lighting in the tent shielded the person's face from view. "I challenge you to a match of strength at the athletic show this evening. Do you accept?"

A murmur of intrigue and amusement rippled through the crowd.

"What's the athletic show?" Carla whispered to Abby.

Before Abby could attempt an answer, Boleslaw intercepted the question, "Never you mind, *mala mysz*."

Carla looked puzzled at the nickname and quite unsatisfied by the answer. She drew her eyebrows together. "Is it illegal? Is that why you won't say?"

Boleslaw laughed. "No! You clever thing. It is legal, but for the grown-ups … And so is the last act, so back out you go." Once again, he lifted the tent flap and hurried the Amaro siblings out, youngest first.

As Abby gathered her younger brothers and sisters, Gregor's voice boomed once more. "Wait! Young man! I did not see you before!"

Natale froze, and Abby's heart stopped.

Chapter Three

Later that night, after the young Amaro siblings had been dropped off at home, and after a series of protests from all of them that they wanted to see, Abby and Natale returned to the carnival. "I don't see why we're doing this," Abby muttered as they approached the tent, which now advertised the night's athletic show. Five tough-looking men, one of whom was Gregor, stood outside on another small raised platform, showing off how much weight they could lift and challenging passersby to a show of strength.

"Because we get two hundred dollars if I win. Don't pretend we can't use that money. It's two weeks' wages."

As they passed the weightlifters and entered the tent, Natale winced, but Abby did not mention it. Natale could fight. He had worked in road construction while putting himself through night school; it left him well-built and able to scrap. Nevertheless, these men had a road-honed strength and looked as though they could rip his head from his shoulders without breaking a sweat.

"You really think you can win?"

"Thanks for the vote of confidence."

The pair took their seats. Natale watched the stage, which had been transformed into a boxing ring, while Abby watched the people entering: men still in their work clothes and laughing women with kerchiefs tied around their necks. Nothing distinguished this crowd from any other in a Cleveland bar on a Saturday night. In the corner near the door stood Boleslaw, his face now devoid of pins. He was talking to a younger woman, who appeared to be closer to Abby's age. When Abby saw her, she couldn't look away. The girl was astonishingly pretty and quite tall. Her hair, a dark auburn color, was tied into an intricately braided bun, and her face, though scrunched into a scowl, showed chiseled features. Her muscular arms were crossed, and she looked quite annoyed by whatever Boleslaw was telling her. "What do you know?!" She shouted and stormed off into the ring.

"Look, Abby," Natale hissed. "Girls can fight too. Go challenge her!"

Abby shook her head. "How about I just try to get a few extra dollars in tips tomorrow? It'd be better for my health."

In the middle of the ring, the young woman lifted a large metal rod, then snapped it in half. The crowd in the tent fell silent, and all eyes turned to face her.

Natale nodded slowly. "Yes, I think you're right."

"Ladies and gentlemen!" she called out. Her voice was strong and carried without any aid. Abby imagined her opera coaches drooling over it. "Tonight, on this stage, you will be witness to great feats, not only of strength, but of cunning, bravery, and will. Those assembled are truly spectacular, but I'm sure that the men of your city might prove to be a challenge. What do you say, folks?"

The assembled crowd roared.

"That's right! Then let's get started. Now, we fight using professional wrestling rules here. I want to assure you, these fights are fair as fair. And first of the night, welcome our own Gregor to the ring!"

Natale sat up straighter as Gregor strode in. Abby bit her lip and tried hard not to feel worried. "What happens now?" she hissed.

Before Natale could answer, Gregor had pointed in their direction. "I see you have accepted my challenge."

Natale glanced around, looking lost and unclear about what to do. Abby wanted to reassure him, but she didn't know what to do either.

Gregor laughed a forced, loud laugh. "Are you scared now or are you going to join me?"

Gulping down a deep breath, Natale stood and made his way through the crowd to the ring. Silently praying that he would come through this alive, Abby clutched her hands together.

The young woman who had opened the event squared Natale and Gregor off in the center of the ring. "Remember, I want a clean and fair fight. Nothing dirty, Gregor, *this* time." Her emphasis on "this" made Abby involuntarily clench her hands more tightly. She held her breath.

"Do you agree to these terms?" the woman asked Natale. He nodded, already sweating.

Then she turned to face Gregor, who looked utterly calm. "Do you—"

Before she could finish the question, Gregor struck out, hitting Natale square in the nose. The audience gasped. Abby jumped to her feet.

Natale stumbled back, trying to get his footing, but Gregor had the momentum. He lashed out, hitting hard and fast. Abby heard herself scream, but she heard it as if she were outside her body, listening to a poorly tuned radio.

"How dare you!" a voice bellowed from the back of the audience, somehow making itself heard over the din of the indignation from the rest of the crowd. "This man is my friend!" The voice continued as the man it belonged to pushed forward through the audience. When he started climbing into the ring, Abby saw that it was none other than Frank Butler. She would have recognized that purposefully rumpled white sport coat anywhere. With what seemed like relative ease, Frank pulled Gregor away from Natale and hit him, knocking the carnival fighter to the ground. He remained there, unmoving.

Natale wobbled. His face was bloody, and he looked close to passing out. Abby raced forward, forgetting for a split second how much she hated Frank. She scrambled into the ring and gathered her brother into her arms.

Frank and the referee stood back, watching. The referee's eyes were wide, their icy blue color accentuating her look of surprise. She took a step forward and stopped with a partly outstretched arm. Something about the way she stood seemed to say she had been frozen by fear. Frank, however, smirked, looking moderately pleased with himself. "Don't worry, Abby, he's going to be fine," Frank said.

More than anything, Abby wanted to shout back that he didn't know that, but instead she shook her head and looked at her brother's bruising face.

Natale coughed and looked at the referee. "I am gonna be fine. No thanks to you. You said clean fight."

She nodded, still looking stricken. "Gregor—"

"You said—"

Abby tugged on Natale's arm to stop him from saying anything more. She wanted to leave. A terrible sense of foreboding had settled inside her since she set foot in that show tent; now it was taking her over. "It doesn't matter anymore, okay? Let's go. Please, Natale?"

The two began to make their way out of the ring.

"Wait!" Frank called after them.

Abby didn't want to stop. She wanted to get home before she even thought about stopping. Natale, however, did stop. He turned back to face Frank. "What is it?"

"I want to talk to Abby. You owe me that much."

Abby turned back as well; her heart seemed to catch with fear. Frank stood at the edge of the ring, holding out a rose. "Abby Amaro, look, I just saved your brother's life. Please marry me?"

"No," she said before thinking. Whether he rescued Natale or not didn't enter into the equation.

"Abby, I think that's a mistake. You need me to protect you."

"No."

"I'm a powerful man, Abby. I would hate to see something happen to you." There was a glint in his eye, one that Abby had seen before. It was a glint that said Frank knew he was going to win a prize. Abby wasn't about to give him that prize. She squeezed Natale's hand to say, "I'm sorry," and bolted from the tent.

When Natale finally found her, huddled behind a shuttered concession stand, a wave of guilt crashed over her. He still looked terrible. His face was even more swollen than it had been just after the fight. "This is all my fault," she muttered when he came into view. "I'm so sorry, Natale."

"How the hell is it your fault?" he asked, helping her to her feet.

"Frank," she spat. "He's behind it somehow. He made that man hurt you."

"You don't know that."

Abby shook her head. She did know that. She didn't know how she knew, but she did. "He all but threatened me, Nate. I… I can't do this anymore. I can't see him anymore."

"And, you don't have to."

"No, Nate, you don't understand. I think I need to get away. I need to get out of Cleveland."

"And go where?"

"I don't know."

The pair stared at each other for a long time, sizing up the situation. Abby could hardly bear to look at her brother's face for fear that she wouldn't be able to keep her resolve. She knew Frank; if he didn't see her, he would lose interest, but if things continued on as they were now, she hated to think of the possible outcomes. If he could inflict such a thing on Natale, she didn't want to think of what he could do to her younger siblings.

She knew they needed her. The younger ones could barely talk to Nonna, and even if Natale could manage them on his own, did she want to do that to him? The family could get by without the little she brought in from the diner, and after all it wouldn't be for long, but where would she go? Her thoughts drifted to her mother's sister, Aunt Teresa in Chicago. She hadn't seen her in years, and they hadn't parted on great terms, but maybe—

Natale took a deep, resigned breath. "Fine," he said, breaking into Abby's thoughts. "Fine. Come on. I didn't want her to see me like this, but … can't be helped."

Puzzled by his words, Abby watched him walk off, then dashed after him. He didn't head toward the car. Instead, he went deeper into the almost empty carnival grounds. All the game booths and concession stands had been closed in anticipation of the next day's move. The entire place had a haunted air.

At the edge of the grounds, they marched through a collection of trucks, wagons, and trailers. Abby rushed forward and clutched his arm, letting go only slightly when he grimaced. "I don't think we're supposed to be here," she whispered.

"We're fine," he hissed back, going up to a trailer that had a garland of feathers over the front door. He rapped hard on the metal frame, which vibrated through the night much louder than Abby would have liked.

"Who's there?" a woman's voice with an obviously faked Swedish accent called out.

"Natale Amaro." There was something off about his voice, a note of sweetness that Abby didn't often hear from him, and then only when dealing with family.

The door flew open. A thin blonde in lacy red lingerie burst from inside the trailer and wrapped her arms around Natale. "Baby! What are you doing here? I thought we already said our goodbyes. You're not gonna try and tag along now, are ya? You know I ain't that kind of girl."

"This isn't for me, Della."

The girl pulled back and looked at Natale's face. Even in the dim light, she seemed able to make out his injuries. "Baby, what happened?"

"Trying my hand at wrestling. Didn't go so well."

Della's face shrank, contorting into a mixture of concern, confusion, and annoyance. "If you're about to tell me that you need to go on the run—"

"No, Della," Natale pressed. He stepped down the trailer stairs to allow Della and Abby a clear view of each other. "My sister does."

The young women stared at each other a long while. Abby had the intense feeling of being appraised, much as she felt with the other girls at the opera. She didn't like it at all.

"Your sister?" Della asked, her voice tense, but trying to sound soft. Natale nodded. "Both of you, then. Come in." She disappeared into the trailer.

Natale gestured for Abby to follow, but her feet felt stuck. This had not been her plan. It took several moments of intense concentration before she managed to move her feet enough to go inside.

Having never been inside a trailer before, Abby didn't know what she had been expecting, but it wasn't quite like this. Every available surface, including the walls, was draped with fabrics, strings of sequins, beads, and feathers. A battered dress dummy loomed ominously in the corner with more pins sticking out of it than Boleslaw's face. Everything seemed to be half-finished, as if once begun a project could only hold Della's attention for so long.

"Excuse the mess," Della said. "We didn't have a show tonight, so I was trying to get some work done." She cleared a partially disassembled, cherry red tulle skirt off some cushions and gestured for Natale and Abby to take a seat. "Need a new costume for Toledo."

Abby stared at the collection of clothing. "Are you a seamstress?"

Della half-laughed, half-coughed. "Suppose I could be if I had to be, gorgeous, but, no, I'm the star of the girl show."

"Girl show?" Abby asked. Then she saw Natale blush and realized exactly what it meant. "Never mind."

"Now, now," Della said, tsking for show. "You mustn't judge your brother too harshly. This softy is my Cleveland sweetheart." She pecked him on the cheek as she sat down across the small table. Then her manner became serious. Her thinly drawn eyebrows pulled close together, and her bright red lips practically disappeared. "Now, tell me what we're in for."

Natale began to tell the story of Abby and Frank Butler, and Abby was grateful that she wouldn't have to be the one to relate it. Her mind was still reeling. She could barely process what had happened, except that it was somehow because of Frank, and that she needed to get out of his sight line to protect her family.

"Ugh, Gregor. I should have guessed. He's been known to pull this kind of thing. Take some side money to rig the fight. Not that I can blame him. You should see that man's medical bills. And, he's got two kids. No offense, baby." She gingerly touched a bruise near his eye, looking sheepish about her defense of Gregor. "You want me to scrounge up some ice for that? The beer garden guy's probably still kicking around out there somewhere."

Natale shook his head. "Nah. I can handle it when I get home, I just … Abby? Can she ride with you a while?"

Della sighed, but didn't answer.

"Just 'til, uh, Kalamazoo or Chicago? This thing should blow over by then. I can tell people she's sick and, when Frank loses interest, meet the show and pick her up."

"And how can we be sure this Frank is gonna lose interest?"

Natale opened his mouth to speak, but it was Abby's turn. "When I started my opera classes, and we didn't see each other every day, it took him all of a week to meet a new girl and forget all about me. And I was still in the same town then."

Della still looked skeptical, but her lips had returned to their normal size and shape. Her eyes were more sympathetic. "Can you do anything? I mean, I can't just hide some possum belly queen in my trailer for a few jumps and hope no one will notice. They watch the food like hawks—unless you don't eat or drink, princess? That too much to ask?"

"I can sing," Abby tried.

"She can sew," Natale added, gesturing at the trailer full of half-finished costumes. Abby tried her best not to look surprised.

Della stood up and paced. Natale tried a few times to add something, but Della just held up her hand, which silenced him immediately. She went to the trailer door and peeked out. Then she turned back and nodded slowly. Both Abby and Natale breathed a sigh of relief.

"On one condition," Della added. "You never put me in her position."

Natale looked confused. "I don't—"

"Never. And I mean, never, Natale. Never ask me to marry you."

He looked stunned at her serious tone, then laughed. "Sure, Del, if that's what you want."

"I'm serious, Natale."

He nodded. It was hard to tell from his face if he was disappointed, but Abby decided not to make any snap judgments.

"Thank you," she said, then stood up. "I can have my things packed in—"

"No can do, sweetie," Della interrupted. "We're making the jump right after they pack up the AT show. You're gonna have to stay put."

~1940~

FOUR-YEAR-OLD ABBY'S FIRST OPERA IS a kaleidoscope of color, a mélange of scents, and flashes of feeling. She grips Nonna Gaetana's hand as they scurry across Euclid Avenue. A gust of wind tries to separate them, and the snow flutters about her face and the looming brick building. Her grandmother whispers the name Carmela Cafarelli with such reverence that young Abby mistakes it for that of a saint.

Abby exults in the music, the arching elegant melodies, the overlapping disparate harmonies, and the high Cs that send shivers through her. The colors of the auditorium itself do not register. She has never heard anything so beautiful and is convinced that the performance did not include humans at all, but an almost pagan mixture of angels and the *donas de fuera,* the mysterious Sicilian fairies her nonna spoke of in hushed tones.

The eggs her mother puts on her plate at breakfast the next morning are light and fluffy as her mother's laugh when Abby tells her, mouth full of frittata, that she is going to be a "soprano."

"Do you even know what that means?" her mother asks. "To be a soprano?"

When Abby doesn't answer, her mother laughs again and goes back to the sink. She sings in a voice that is much thinner than the women Nonna Gaetana took Abby to see, but sweet and lovely in its own way: "*Vinni la primavera li mennuli sù n'ciuri. Lu focu di l'ammuri lu cori m'addurmò.*"

Spring has come; almond trees are in blossom; the fire of love took over my heart.

Chapter Four

Abby couldn't remember falling asleep. She only remembered the dark night and how, outside the window of Della's trailer, the rolling slopes of eastern Ohio slowly flattened into the farmland of the western side of the state and faded into darkness. She didn't say much during the trip, but her mind was spinning, unable to process what she had done.

Once, when she was a little girl, barely older than Annette was now, her mother had taken her and Natale to visit their aunt in Chicago for a week. It had been a nice visit. They had embarked on the train with a great deal of ceremony, and Za Teresa had spoiled the pair rotten, loading them up with peach-shaped marzipan and pizzelle until they were both sick. She hadn't left Cleveland for any extended period of time since. Oh, sure, she'd talked and dreamt about it. Nonna often wistfully mentioned taking a trip back to her girlhood home one more time now that the war was over and taking Abby along to look after her, and then, if Abby's opera career took off as she had once hoped, she would be visiting all the great cities. In her scrapbook, clippings of Palais Garnier, La Scala, and The Met were decorated with carefully drawn hearts and hopeful stars and the scrawled word: *someday*. Still, she had never imagined that when she departed the Coventry neighborhood again, it would be in a burlesque dancer's trailer.

She woke to the sound of a window scraping open. All at once, she heard the clattering sounds of hammers on metal blended with a buzz of people shouting to be heard over one another. It took Abby a moment to remember where she was. Taking a deep breath, she opened her eyes. Della was leaning over her.

"There," Della said, moving back from the window. "We've got to get some air moving in here or we'll be baked alive."

"How long have I been asleep?" Abby muttered. Now instead of wide open fields, Abby saw a cluster of trucks and trailers. Men and women of all shapes and sizes milled about, carrying boxes, tall poles, and canvas rolls. "What's happening?"

"You missed breakfast," Della said, setting a small packet of folded napkins on Abby's lap. "Probably for the best for now, but I managed to sneak out some blueberries. Told them I was gonna feed the birds."

Abby opened the packet and popped one of the blueberries into her mouth. "I suppose it would be too much to hope for some coffee?"

Della leveled a steely-eyed frown in her direction; Abby nodded and went back to her blueberries.

"I'll talk to McClure this afternoon," Della suggested as she rummaged through a drawer beneath her bed. The clothes she removed from it seemed far more functional as everyday wear than the piles of tulle, chiffon, and feathers that still decorated the table and much of the floor. She tossed a red and white polka-dotted shirtwaist dress in Abby's direction. "See if I can get you a tryout for the girl show."

"I don't think—"

"It's a little outdated, sure, but I think it should fit, and if you need to give it some volume—"

"I'm not talking about the dress, Della. I'm sure it's fine." Abby held the dress up for inspection. Style-wise it was quite similar to the uniform she wore at the diner, only red instead of pink, but it looked too small. One glance at Della and she was almost certain that it was. Della was petite, but while she and Abby were about the same height, that was one of the few places their figures matched. Abby could already foresee a struggle with the row of buttons down the front. She swallowed hard, unsure if she would make it to Kalamazoo if she had only Della's clothes to wear. "You wouldn't happen to have an extra girdle, would you?"

Della didn't seem to hear her. She pulled a few pins out of her dress dummy and adjusted the drape of filmy red fabric around the base.

Abby sighed and set the dress down, once again returning to her blueberry breakfast. "And, about the—well, I'm not a prude. I just don't think I'm comfortable letting other people see me naked, is all."

Della gathered up a string of purple beads and tried them around the dummy's waist. Then, without warning, she began to laugh. "Oh, princess, the fact that you're not from a theater family is going to take some getting used to."

"Excuse me?"

"You're afraid to change while I'm in the trailer?"

"No, I—" That wasn't what she had been referring to at all. She took a deep breath watching Della. It almost seemed as if she were skirting the issue on purpose.

Della tried hard to stifle her giggles, but they kept bubbling through. "Oh, poor little sheltered princess—"

"I do theater, you know," Abby protested. "I study opera at the Cleveland Institute! It's very prestigious."

"I'm sure it is, precious. I didn't mean to imply anything." Della took a deep breath and patted Abby on the arm in a mock calming gesture. "I, however, did vaudeville from the age of two, traveling the country with my parents. It's a little different. You get a certain level of comfort with people."

Abby eyed her suspiciously and shrugged. "That dress isn't going to fit anyway."

Della waved her hand. "So you got a little more going on upstairs than I do. The boys'll love how much it clings."

"I'm sure I—well, the whole—not just 'upstairs'—" Abby paused and took a breath before starting again. "I don't like to be looked at," she finally managed to force out. "And I don't want to be a part of your show either. I'm sorry, but I'm not exactly—"

"Exactly what?" Her eyebrows leveled once again, Della turned back to Abby. Her expression wasn't quite a glare, but it wasn't far from becoming one either.

"You know ..."

"No, I don't. Enlighten me."

Abby looked down at her blueberries, but she could still feel Della's eyes watching her, evaluating. She felt sick to her stomach. "I just ... it's not for me."

She could almost feel the roll of Della's eyes. "Do you want to live on blueberries?"

"No. I already miss coffee."

Della laughed; the ice was suddenly gone from her voice. Abby wondered if it were truly gone or if she was just very good at covering her anger. "Then we need to find you a purpose. A carnival doesn't run with extra parts."

"Well, Natale told you that I can sew." This was a lie, of course, but she was willing to give it a try if it meant getting a cup of coffee. It wouldn't matter if it were instant. She wasn't going to be picky.

"Which is why I let you come in my trailer. That ain't gonna be enough for the McClures if they find you hanging around."

Abby puzzled over this, allowing her eyes to flick around the trailer, hoping to catch a sudden jolt of inspiration. All she could see were mountains of tulle. "Well, I... I may have mentioned last night that I sing."

Della waved a hand. "People don't come to a carnival to hear some girl sing *Carmen*." She paused and smirked. "See? I know things."

"They don't?"

"No. They don't. You want to be a singer, you go join a Broadway show or something, Miss Rogers and Hammerstein. Your usual lot lice are looking for something more—"

"I don't see why not. I mean—"

"No!" The vehemence in her voice stopped Abby cold. The pair stared at each other; Della seemed to dare her to protest one last time. When she didn't, Della gave a decisive nod. "Right then. I'll go talk to McClure. Maybe we can get you on the bally or something, if you're really that uncomfortable with what I do." Then she slipped out her door after flashing a look that Abby hoped was more sympathetic than pitying. She couldn't be sure.

Abby watched the aluminum trailer door for a few minutes after Della left. When she was certain she had gone, she returned to her blueberries, still trying her best to ignore the dress. The trailer was sweltering. Her head felt as if it were being boiled in some sort of stew; something spicy and filled with cannellini beans, one of her favorites. Then, for a split second, instead of a blueberry, she tasted the sweet almond flavor of marzipan. Puzzled, she popped another into her mouth, but this one tasted exactly the way a blueberry was supposed to.

"I've got to get out of here," she whispered to herself.

The air outside the trailer wasn't much better than the air inside. The day was hot and humid with a relentless sun, but at least there was movement. Every so often a tent would go up, sending a wave of man-made breeze in Abby's direction. Her mind still felt as if it were bobbing in a pot of minestrone, but at least she wasn't cooped up. All around her, people bustled this way and that, speaking quickly, shouting words that only half sounded like English.

"Cut it with the gaff, Bobby! This here's a Sunday school show!"

"One of them candy butchers blew the route around Amherst. You're on your own!"

Some of the words weren't English at all. They were German or Spanish or Russian or other tongues that Abby couldn't begin to place.

Something inside her felt deeply displaced, like a book put on the wrong shelf, and she wondered if Nonna Gaetana and her father had felt this way when they arrived in Cleveland all those years ago. At least they'd had their family with them.

Trying to tune out the commotion, she carefully picked her way through the vendors, who were in various states of setup. "Not yet, miss," one of the game operators called out to her as she walked past his booth. He appeared to be filling a small pool of water, and Abby recognized it as one of the games she and Natale wouldn't let Annette and Carla play. The prize had been a choice of bunnies, and they had begged and begged. "Where in the world would we put it?" she had asked the younger girls. Now she wished she had let them try to win the rabbits. It wasn't as though she would be home to deal with them after all.

At the end of the midway, she found that at least one ride's setup was complete: the haunted train. Once again, she heard Annette's voice, "Pleeease can we go again, Abbbyyy? Pleeease?"

Her walk down memory lane was interrupted by the ride operator, who leaned out of his booth and said, "Would you like to take the inaugural ride, Miss?"

Abby startled, but only briefly. When she turned to face him, she laughed. Maybe it was his out-of-place ringmaster's top hat or simply his voice, but something about him immediately reminded her of someone she had seen before. After a split second she decided that he must have been a customer at the diner when they were in Cleveland, or perhaps he just looked a little like Roman around the eyes. What would Natale tell the diner staff about what had happened to her and where she had gone? "Nothing else looks ready yet."

He puffed his chest out proudly. "No, but that's where I have an advantage. I set up right when we arrive. No matter how late it is. No rest for the wicked. Plus," he said, eying her as if she made his point by standing there, "there's always one or two townies that mill about early. It pays to be the only one running."

"That it does." She dug a few coins out of her skirt pocket and bought herself a ticket. The operator began the ride and saluted as the train chugged into its tunnel. "Keep your hands and feet inside the ride at all times," he called out as the outside world disappeared from view.

She had hoped for a diner-like effect, but to no avail. The inside of the ride looked darker and gloomier than Abby remembered. She had ridden the train twice the day before and could easily anticipate the robotic zombies and motion-activated chain rattles, so it wasn't exactly frightening. Rather, it made her feel cold and empty. The rubber spiders that hung from the ceiling of the tunnel seemed more obviously fake than they had when Carla had been cowering from them in the bottom of her train car. A feeling of disappointment came over her as she watched sheets meant to be ghosts drift by. She experienced no distraction at all from her real-life problems. Then, toward the end of the ride, a series of flashing strobe lights rendered her practically blind. She had barely noticed them yesterday. She had been too busy comforting her younger siblings. Today, however, they terrified her.

Abby screamed and ducked her head into her lap, trying to blot out the sensation that accompanied not being able to see. It didn't help.

The ride screeched to a stop. It was over. Now, she was outside and safe. Still, her heart pounded wildly.

"Scary, huh?" the ride operator teased, holding out a hand to help her from the train car.

She avoided his hand but nodded, not wanting to explain how she really felt about the ride. Instead, she gulped down air and attempted to walk away with as much dignity as possible. That dignity didn't last long. After she had walked a few steps, a sudden, blistering-hot wave of dizziness and nausea came over her. She would either faint or be sick. She raced forward, forgetting her pride, simply trying to get away from people, but there were people everywhere. Everywhere she turned, someone else was assisting with a booth or carting around a large tub of potatoes. Overcome, she dropped onto a picnic bench. The tears came before she could stop them.

"Are you all right?" a young woman's voice, one with a familiar-sounding eastern Ohio accent, asked.

Abby nodded, wiping furiously at her eyes. She didn't want to be caught crying.

"Are you sure?"

"Yes, I'm fine."

The young woman didn't leave. Instead, she sat down on the bench next to Abby, and, though she didn't dare look, Abby could tell her eyes were watching her. "It can be a lot to take in. I've been with the troupe for a while myself, and I still have days …" She trailed off, and Abby finally risked looking at her. She was soft-featured, with dark brown eyes that reminded her of Nonna Gaetana's. There was a warmth there, a welcoming expression that seemed to say, "It's okay if you don't fit. I don't either. That's the point."

"How do you know I'm not just some—what was it Della called them? Lot lice?"

The young woman laughed. Abby was pleased to hear honesty in it. "My name's Ruth," she said, standing up and holding out a hand.

Abby took it and got to her feet. "And I'm Abby. Just Abby. Not Abigail."

"Noted. Now, did you say that you were friends with Della?" She paused; her face looked as if she were searching for a word. "What's her last name, Adamson?"

"'Friend might be a strong word," Abby explained. "I suppose I'm more her ward."

Ruth looked briefly both puzzled and disappointed, but did not comment. "Come along then. Let's get you better acquainted with the place."

Chapter Five

As Ruth led her through the maze of games and concessions, Abby's dizziness decreased ever so gradually. "If you ever hear anybody refer to someone else as a 'jockey,' they mean a ride operator," Ruth explained, gesturing toward a group of people attempting to hammer into place a track of spinning carriages shaped like strawberries. "I'm not sure why. Probably has something to do with carousels, but don't hold me to that."

Abby nodded, taking it all in. Finally, she felt able to take a full breath and look around at the carnival as it unfurled before her.

"The McClures are the owners. They pick the route, but it's up to the advance man, his name is Thomas, to arrange everything, find an appropriate lot, set up a post office box to get mail, make sure we're good with local law enforcement, and all that. Then there's the lot managers. Boleslaw is the one I'm most familiar with. He's in charge of the sideshows, but there are other managers for rides and concessions and …" She trailed off watching Abby's face, which Abby was sure looked more than a little overwhelmed. It was as if she were back in high school and about to be tested on something she would never be able to commit to memory. "It's not as complicated as it seems, but it can take some getting used to. Don't worry. You'll be in orbit before you realize it."

They stopped off at a few food vendors, and Ruth collected sodas, fried vegetables, bratwurst, and calzones which she carefully added to a box. Abby waited patiently, listening as Ruth introduced each vendor by name and hoping she wouldn't notice how wobbly the smells made her feel. "How did you know I wasn't a townie?" she asked after they had been walking for a while. It didn't seem like the kind of thing Della would tell everyone.

Ruth didn't answer. She gestured toward a large open space in front of them. As they approached, and almost as if it sensed their presence, a tent of black-and-red-striped canvas began to rise from the ground.

"That's the show tent," Ruth said, as if it needed explaining.

Abby nodded. Even if she hadn't seen it just yesterday, she would have known it in an instant. The red and black spiral of stripes screamed out a secret code, one that Abby didn't fully understand yet, but even a town girl could get the gist. It said, "Step right up! Something unique is to be seen here! This is your only chance!"

"Come on in then. You should meet everyone."

"No," Abby said, without knowing why. "I can't."

Ruth stared at her. Her expression—head cocked, eyebrows narrowed but eyes widened—could really only be described as one of offended bewilderment. "You're going to have to meet them if you're going to do the bally."

Abby felt terrified at the prospect of meeting the other performers. Ride operators and concessions sales folk were one thing, but this was a different breed. Her mind kept flying back to Boleslaw and his face full of pins, how if it hadn't been for him, she wouldn't have been in this mess in the first place. Or would she? Sooner or later, she would have had to deal with Frank's demands. If it hadn't been the scene at the athletic show, it could have been something much worse.

"Just don't tell them how boring I am," Abby muttered.

Ruth smiled, but said nothing as she took her hand and led her inside the tent.

Just as the rest of the carnival had, the crowd inside the tent looked busy. In the front, a group pieced together the raised platform that had acted as a stage. Others held lights to help with this process. Still others arranged seats and hung garlands.

"I brought lunch!" Ruth called out, setting her box on a nearby bench. Countless unfamiliar faces turned and hurried forward.

"Ruuuth!" a shrill child's voice, much like Annette's, cried from among the throng. Abby turned to see a flash of red-orange hair hurtling toward them.

"Miss Phebe, what are you doing out of the trailer? I don't think Papa will be pleased." Ruth gathered the girl into her arms and stroked her curls back from her forehead. As she did so, Abby could see that the girl's face was covered in downy hair, which was cut back everywhere except her chin where it had been allowed to grow into a long auburn beard. Abby's eyes widened, but she tried her best not to show surprise. She had not seen this little girl yesterday.

"It's boooriiing there," Phebe whined. "Mr. Lambrinos says I'm not allowed to touch anything. Not even the playing cards!"

Her tone and inflections sounded so much like Annette's that Abby had to stifle a laugh. When the little girl heard it, she shrank back in Ruth's arms.

"No, no, baby," Ruth said, cooing and stroking the little girl's curls. "Abby wasn't laughing at you." Though she did flash a look back at Abby, as if to say, "You weren't, were you? Because we can no longer be friends if you were."

Abby shook her head, stooping to the little girl's level as Ruth set her down. She hesitated, then said, "It's just that you remind me of my little sister."

"*I* remind you of your little sister?" Phebe asked, her voice skeptical, betraying a world-weariness that Abby found hard to believe was issuing from a girl no older than eight.

"Well, sisters. There are two of them. Annette and Carla. Carla's closer to your age, but Annette ..." Abby's voice caught. A hollow feeling wormed its way through her stomach as she thought of her sisters. Mentally, she scolded herself. It had been less than a day since she last saw them: far too soon to miss them.

Phebe touched Abby's arm and looked carefully at her face. Abby swallowed hard to quell any tears the little girl might be seeing there. "You miss them?"

Abby allowed herself to nod.

"It's okay to miss them. Mr. Lambrinos says we're allowed to miss people. Even the ones who abandoned us."

The word "abandoned" struck Abby hard. Before she knew what she was doing, she had wrapped her arms around Phebe and pulled her into a hug. She herself hadn't been abandoned; she had done the abandoning. Still, hearing Phebe say it made her feel more alone than she had when her mother died.

Eventually, she felt Phebe gently, awkwardly pat her on the shoulder and whisper "There, there." Flushed with embarrassment, she let go and stood, brushing herself off. Activity in the tent had stopped. All eyes were on her. Only two words popped into her mind: *Damn it.*

Her vision began to narrow, as if the world were growing dark around the edges. The terror that had crept over her in the haunted train was coming back. There were no strobe lights, but the same blindness descended quickly. What had she done? She'd walked away from her family, from her sisters and brothers, from her father in his lonely little world, from her grandmother, even from the career that her grandmother had led her to. Now where was she going? The train had gone off onto a new course.

She wanted to flee, to turn and run from the tent as fast as her feet could carry her, but no matter how many times she sent her legs the signal to run, they stayed firmly rooted.

"Is she all right?" another young woman's voice asked behind her. Ruth made a small noise of uncertainty. Still, Abby couldn't turn to face them. "Do you need anything to drink?" the voice continued. "It is a little hot out today."

Abby closed her eyes and counted slowly. *Una, dui, tri, quattru, cincu*. She turned to face Ruth and another young woman, whom she instantly recognized as the girl with the burning hula hoop. She was dressed in work clothes, baggy green denim overalls and an even baggier grey blouse. Her black hair was tied back in a bandanna, but Abby had seen her put out a fire with her hand; it would have been hard to forget her face.

"I'm fine, thank you," she said, trying to sound poised and calm.

Though neither of them seemed to believe this, Abby was relieved that they didn't press the matter.

"This is Constance, by the way," Ruth said, slipping her arm around the other girl's waist.

Abby looked at them and couldn't help but smile at the way they seemed to fit together like puzzle pieces. Abby wondered if they were sisters, but then she noticed the look in Ruth's eyes. The love there wasn't sisterly. It was a much more fiery affection. Abby had seen that look many a time before, over malted milkshakes and French fries at the diner and between Gregory Peck and Audrey Hepburn in *Roman Holiday*. She hadn't expected to see it exchanged between Constance and Ruth, and yet, the moment she recognized it, the love was obvious. Abby tried not to blush. "Yeah, the fire dancer. I remember you."

"So you've seen the show?" Constance asked. She sounded excited, like when Sal was about to ask Abby how she liked a new dish that he had invented.

"Well, part of it ..."

"She's Della's friend," Ruth explained. "I heard her talking to McClure about getting her on the bally."

"That's wonderful! It would be great to have a woman out there."

Abby watched the two of them, the ease with which they talked, the sweet gentle way they touched and looked each other in the eye. For the first time in a long time, something inside her whispered, "I want someone to look at me like that." She blinked at the thought, forced it down, and allowed herself to ask, "I'm sorry, but no one's told me yet … what's a bally?"

Constance laughed, and Ruth gently tapped her on the forearm. "Don't," she said. "I didn't know either."

"The ballyhoo!" Constance said, with a bright smile. "The one who gets them in the tent. You're the one who stands outside and says 'Step right up and see sights that will delight and amaze!' and things of that sort."

Instead of responding with the excitement she was certain Constance expected, Abby whispered, "Oh, no—"

"It's just talking, really."

"Oh, no," Abby repeated, shaking her head. Her brain filled with images from the opera: stepping to the edge of the stage to audition her pieces; her voice going flat and hoarse, though a moment before it was fine; and, worst of all, the grim, annoyed expressions worn by the music directors.

"I'm a waitress. I'm just a waitress."

"I think she may faint," Ruth whispered to Constance. She took Abby by the arm and guided her toward a chair. "You need to get some food in you. Did you have any breakfast?"

"What seems to be the trouble?" asked yet another voice, male, older, with a heavy Eastern European accent.

Abby groaned inwardly. She didn't want to be the subject of this much attention.

Then, the voice seemed startled. "Miss Amaro?"

Abby jerked her head up and saw Boleslaw holding Phebe by the hand. It looked as though the little girl had dragged him over to help.

Abby shook her head, not to deny who she was, but simply to clear the cobwebs. Part of her knew that she should have expected to see Boleslaw sometime, but she didn't expect the memories of the night before to flood back. At least it wasn't Gregor, though he was surely around as well.

"Miss Amaro, what are you doing here?" he asked again. The heaviness in his voice seemed to have dissipated.

Abby didn't want to answer. She knew it wasn't fair, but she didn't trust Boleslaw. He had brought her brother into the sideshow. The outcome wasn't his fault, yet part of Abby wasn't willing to accept that.

Constance answered for her. "She's traveling with Della Adamson."

Boleslaw still looked puzzled, but seemed willing to take Constance at her word. He opened his mouth, but before Abby heard any words yet another voice rang out.

"There you are!"

For a terrible second, Abby's mind concocted an image of Frank bursting into the tent; however, that image faded quickly. From the other side of the stage came the referee from the night before. Rage burned behind her eyes. Abby appreciated seeing it. Though her own rage had been smothered by nerves and confusion, it made that angry part of her that didn't want to talk to Boleslaw feel validated.

"Suprema," Boleslaw said in a placating voice as he intercepted her. "I've been here the whole time. You know this."

She crossed her arms across her chest and held Boleslaw in an intense glare. "I have things we need to discuss."

"Of course. Let me just finish with Miss Amaro here—"

"Now!"

Boleslaw flashed an apologetic glance at Abby, then nodded toward Suprema. "We can talk outside."

He started toward the exit, but Suprema hung back. She glanced at Abby, then at Constance and Ruth, with a sneer that seemed to yearn to make someone else as angry as she felt. "You've really got to stop collecting the lot lice, Lambrinos," she said, disdain hanging in her voice. "It's starting to look, frankly, pathetic."

"Don't you talk to her like that!" Ruth protested, immediately on her feet. Abby squirmed. Suprema could probably snap Ruth's neck without breaking a sweat, but the look on Ruth's face seemed fierce enough to knock Suprema out on its own.

However, she calmed immediately when Constance touched her elbow. "Not worth it," she whispered.

Suprema smirked and continued on her way. Abby looked quickly at Ruth and Constance: Ruth was still seething. Constance, however, had a perfectly serene expression, despite having been the one insulted.

"Who… who was that?" Abby asked hesitantly, not wanting to break the silent communication that seemed to be passing between Ruth and Constance, but eager to know.

"Suprema," Constance said. Nothing in her face indicated, in any way, how she felt about her. Abby marveled at the skill. "She does a Wonder Woman-type act. Weight lifting, arm wrestling, that kind of thing."

"And she's the referee for the athletic show," Abby whispered.

Constance and Ruth seemed taken aback. "Yes, she is," Constance said. "How did you—"

"It's not important."

Constance regarded her with an appraising air. The calm in her eyes actually gave Abby a small fright. She suddenly wanted very much not to disappoint her.

"My brother competed," she said.

The change in Constance's eyes was almost imperceptible. Behind the calm veneer a brief flash of enlightenment flickered, and she glanced at Ruth, who frowned slightly, but nodded. "Look, I don't mean to pry into your business," Constance said. "I know most folks around here aren't too big on sharing their stories, but if you're who we're thinking, then I wouldn't go after Suprema. She's strong, and she can be a bit abrasive at times, but no more so than your friend Della. And besides, that wasn't her fault."

"But I wasn't—"

"Everyone here has a reason and a story and their own motivations. Suprema's is …"

"Sad," Phebe's small voice piped up. She had gone over to the food box, dug up a few of the remaining tidbits and held a still-warm calzone out to Abby, who took it gratefully. "She definitely has a sad one. She didn't tell me, but I hear things. Only Boleslaw knows all about it, and that's 'cause he's her uncle."

Constance nodded once to acknowledge Phebe and added, in a protective but still eerily calm voice, "I've seen her break a man's arm with her bare hands. I really wouldn't try messing with her about something that wasn't her fault, all right?"

Abby nodded. She hadn't actually been considering anything of the sort. She remembered the look of horror on Suprema's face the night before. She hadn't known what was going to happen any more than Abby or Natale had. That wasn't why Abby wanted to know about Suprema. It had more to do with the way she captivated her attention every time she entered the room and left a void when she departed. Still, there was no use arguing with Constance. It seemed like something that would be difficult to explain. She wasn't even able to explain it to herself.

"Is there anything else we can get you?" Ruth changed the subject. "The first couple days are always a little rocky, but you've got help, so anything you need …"

Abby's gut instinct was to say, "No, I'm fine," but then her eyes happened to settle on the frayed hem of her cotton skirt. "Actually, um, this is the only outfit I have."

Ruth and Constance exchanged glances. "We can probably scrounge something up," Ruth suggested. "If not from either of us, then somewhere. There's plenty of people around, performers, workers, wives. We'll get you fixed up."

A swell of relief drifted over Abby as the idea of wearing the impossibly small red polka-dotted dress vanished from her mind. "I'm an 18 in the Sears catalog. If that helps at all."

Chapter Six

When Ruth and Constance dropped her at Della's trailer—with her meager, newly acquired collection of clothes—Abby found the door locked. She rapped hard on the aluminum door and it vibrated. "I'm coming! I'm coming!" Della answered, emphasizing her fake accent, but when she opened the door and saw Abby standing before her, she sighed with relief. Then she forced her features into a frown. "Oh. I thought you'd run off," she said, the accent gone.

"Sorry to disappoint you," Abby replied, slipping inside. The explosive mess of clothing seemed to have gotten worse since the morning. She kicked a pile of feathered boas aside so that she could step through to the table and set her own bundle down.

Della shrugged, sighing theatrically. She grabbed one of the white and silver boas from the ground, wrapped it around her neck, and plopped down at the small table across from Abby. "You're lucky you caught me. I've got a show in a half hour. You would have had to wait out there in the rain."

"It's not raining."

"It could start. You never know. Makes for a more dramatic story."

Abby considered her for a long moment, unsure whether or not she should laugh. She wanted to ask how things went with McClure, whether or not she was going to be allowed to eat breakfast tomorrow, if this whole thing was going to work, but she couldn't bring herself to speak.

"You gonna come to the show, then?" Della asked, breaking the silence. She pulled on a pair of bright red pumps, pointed her foot, and admired her ankle.

"I don't know."

"C'mon. It's not like you're gonna have to demean yourself by actually performing or anything." Though her tone was sarcastic, Abby could sense resentment.

"It's not that, I just … wasn't I meant to be hiding out?"

Della raised a skeptical eyebrow. Abby couldn't blame her. She had, after all, spent the whole day wandering around the carnival with the sideshow performers. Surely, by now, most everyone had seen her. "You've never been to a burlesque, have you?" she asked.

Abby wasn't sure how to respond. She had walked into a minefield, and no matter whether her answer was, "No I haven't," which was the truth, or, "Yes I have," which wasn't, Della had the perfect sarcastic retort planned. She let Della's words hang in the air and pretended, badly, not to have heard.

"I figured as much." Della smiled; her features turned warm and motherly as she took Abby by the arm. The expression looked out of place on her, somehow. "We can't have this. If you're going to feel at home here at McClure's Traveling Amusements, then you're going to have to truly experience it."

Abby wanted to protest, but part of her did concede that point. "I suppose—"

"It's settled then." Della stood, tugging Abby to her feet as well. "I promise you won't—well, no, I can't promise that. You might regret it, but isn't life really all about taking chances?"

The "Girl Show" tent was dark when Della led her inside. "Looks like we're the first ones," she said brightly, kicking around on the floor. "There should be a cord down here somewhere."

Though Abby wasn't sure what she was supposed to be looking for, she glanced back and forth, at least pretending to be helpful. Seconds later, the tent came to life, and Abby gasped. Hundreds of fairy lights were strung between the tent poles. They gave the space an ethereal glow.

"Nice, isn't it?" Della said. "We were using big theater lights on the poles, but they make everything too bright and they really washed me out, so then I saw something like this in a picture of some place in Rome and I went straight to Mrs. McClure."

Abby nodded as Della went on, detailing her other aesthetic choices, from plants in turquoise pots at the edge of the audience seating area to the red drape pinned up in front of the stage. A voice inside her doubted that Della had come up with all of these things, but she tried hard to force it down. She had known Della for less than twenty-four hours, and, while she did seem rather scattered, her desire for style was clear from her costumes.

"So this is where you dance, then?" Abby asked, if only to stop Della from describing the artistic value of the straw-covered ground.

Della paused, looking somewhat sardonic. "I don't really dance. What I do is better."

Abby's stomach squirmed. "Never mind then."

It seemed Della could sense this discomfort, as she grinned in triumph. "You should stop thinking you know what to expect around here, Abigail. It's not becoming."

Abby didn't bother to correct her about her name.

"Some of the other girls dance. They should be here any minute. No time to meet them though, 'cause so should the crowd. Maybe after?"

A woman in a crisp suit dress, pillbox hat, and pumps, all of which were purple, pulled back the curtain. She studied Abby, then gave an almost imperceptible shrug. "Done with the tour, Della? We're just waiting on you and Vivian."

Della glanced around. Feet could be seen shuffling about just outside the tent. She looked embarrassed. It was the first time Abby had seen such an emotion on Della's face. "Oh, wow, look at the time. Sorry, Mrs. McClure."

"Tell your friend to have a seat." She smiled elegantly at both Abby and Della in turn, and then stepped behind the curtain with the kind of flourish Abby had only seen in movies.

"That's Mrs. McClure?" Abby whispered, eyes wide. "She could be Vivian Leigh!"

Della nodded. "Isn't she beautiful?"

"She's stunning."

Again, Della nodded, her eyes clouded. "She used to be a burlesque dancer, too. Took me in after I ran off and found a way for me to work in the show. No questions asked about anything." She laughed in an odd, bitter way. "Taught me better than my let's-have-eight-babies-just-cause-the menfolk-are-finally-home mother would have ever managed."

Abby forced a smile, because she knew Della was attempting to tell a joke. "My family's pretty much the s— "

"Anyway, neither here nor there. You should sit down. You're in for a real treat."

Before Abby could ask any further about Mrs. McClure or even inquire as to where she should sit, Della had vanished behind the curtain and a slow but steady stream of people was filing into the tent.

Hoping not to be noticed, Abby shrank into a seat near the back corner. The crowd was small, but the people all seemed riled up and fully able to cause plenty of trouble. One man had begun throwing popcorn at the stage before he even sat down. She tried not to think of them, but focused on the stage like a horse with blinders and imagined herself enveloped in her own cocoon. She longed for the safety of the diner.

The first act, a young woman with bright red hair introduced as Trixie Rose, performed a comedic routine reminiscent of *I Love Lucy*, except that her movements were more explicitly sensual and her circle skirt always seemed to fall just above her thighs when she sat or pretended to faint. Abby was surprised by how amusing she found the whole routine.

After she rushed off the stage, darkness fell. It seemed to chasten the crowd, which had been whistling and chanting raucously. Without introduction, a young woman who could have been the twin of Lena Horne, carrying only a single candle, walked to the center of the stage. She looked like a goddess, draped in white linen. "Vivian," someone nearby whispered. The whisper rippled through the room like an announcement.

When the rustle of her name died down, she began to speak, reciting poetry, both romantic and erotic. No one spoke. The audience barely dared to move. Then, just as she had come onto the stage, she exited—only stark naked, leaving the linen drape behind.

Music jarred everyone out of the mystical spell Vivian had created: a tinny-sounding record, probably playing on an old player offstage. It was a lively tune, but it took Abby almost a full minute to pinpoint the voice as belonging to Perry Como. Two girls scurried onto the stage, Trixie Rose and a brunette Abby hadn't seen before, both moving their hips in a mockery of the hula. They were clad as Della had been, in barely visible skin-tight leotards covered in strategically placed sparkles and spangles of red and white, but they lacked her feather boa.

The song went on with the girls shimmying provocatively and blowing kisses to the hoots and hollers of the audience, until, almost as if a wind had changed, Perry Como's voice stopped beckoning for a mambo, and a booming voice echoed, "And now, ladies and gentlemen, our one and only Princess of the Sky, Miss Adelaide!"

A single violin began to play a mournful melody. The wolf whistles died away as the girls stepped to one side and Della walked to center stage from the back. A ring lowered from the ceiling. With a wink to the audience, she strung her feather boa through the ring and held on tight as it slowly lifted high above the stage. Abby held her breath. She had once panicked on a stepladder. The entire room was silent, except the violin.

Abby stared. Speechless.

"Something, isn't she?" asked a woman's voice from behind her. Abby spun quickly. There, leaning against a pole, sipping from a small silver flask, was Mrs. McClure. Suddenly, Abby felt guilty, though she couldn't say about what.

"Yes, yes she is."

Mrs. McClure held the flask in Abby's direction and took a seat next to her. Without a second thought, Abby took a drink from the flask and handed it back. The whiskey burned in her throat. She watched as Mrs. McClure took a long drink while appraising the reaction of the crowd with a satisfied look. "They all are. Honestly. Very talented. And not just for this show. For the whole thing. We don't take on the mediocre."

There it was. Abby recognized her guilt with a rush of heat. Mrs. McClure knew who she was, that she was freeloading with Della. "I—I'm sorry, Mrs. McClure …"

Shaking her head, she pressed a finger to her lips.

High above the stage, Della had kicked off her pumps and begun to propel herself in circles. Those below were still utterly silent. As she spun, in tighter and tighter circles, the violin's song grew faster and more frantic. Then, as it reached a fever pitch, she let go. The entire room held its breath. She somersaulted once, then hit the stage with a bow.

Abby couldn't help herself. As the room erupted into applause and shouting, she joined in, carried away by it. Roses were thrown onstage, and Della picked them up, cooing in her fake accent, "Oh, thank you. It was nothing. Honestly, nothing. I was not good today. You should see the act tomorrow. Now that will really be something." Then she blew a kiss and left the other girls to their record—this time Peggy Lee.

Chapter Seven

After the show, Abby glanced around for Mrs. McClure, but she had drifted away. The thrill of seeing the show fled her mind as she rushed through the exiting crowd to find Della, hoping against hope that she could get back to the trailer before Mrs. McClure had her thrown out.

The girls were behind the tent. Trixie Rose and the brunette were wrapped under a wool navy blanket, taking turns with a single cigarette. Vivian and Della, however, were both already dressed for a night out in matching yellow and purple sheath dresses with sweetheart collars. If Abby hadn't been so frantic, she would have found this amusing. Della did not seem to be the sort of person who would allow anyone to wear a dress that matched hers if she had any say in the matter.

"There you are!" Della called out. "I was worried you got lost."

Abby shrugged off the warm reception. "We have to go," she said, taking Della by the wrist.

Della just smiled, looking amused. "Not even gonna tell us how good we were?"

"Mrs. McClure—"

"Thinks you're very pretty and will be quite a draw for the bally," Della finished, patting Abby's hand until she let go of her wrist.

"I—"

The other girls burst into a laugh that sounded cruel to Abby's ears, and Della shook her head. "I told them you were a touch excitable."

"I'm not—" but Abby stopped trying to defend herself.

Again, the four of them laughed. Abby had the distinct feeling that she was backstage at the opera, listening to the other girls laugh over an inside joke directed at her. Her stomach squirmed. Her stomach had been doing an awful lot of squirming today, and she didn't like it at all.

"We're going for drinks. We always go for drinks," Della said as the laughter died away. "And you're coming."

Abby wanted to shake her head, but she knew nothing she said would dissuade Della. It would be "Are you coming to my show?" all over again. So she took a deep breath and forced a smile. Della seemed to take this as an encouraging sign. She linked her arm through Abby's and started to lead her away.

"We'll meet you there!" Vivian called after them. "Someone's got to look after these two."

Della waved to acknowledge her.

"And where are we going?" Abby asked.

"Could you not have a cow in front of the girls, please?" was all Della would say.

It wasn't until two cocktails in that Abby got up the courage to mention how impressive she found Della's act.

Della scoffed, though her eyes sparkled. "It's no big deal."

"No big deal?" Abby asked. "I could never do something like that."

"Well, I should say not." Della waved to a passing busboy and raised her empty glass. He seemed to get the hint. "You were born on the ground like most. Not your fault, just your lot in life."

Normally, Abby would have brushed this off. She had been brushing off Della's jabs all day. However, she was getting quite tired of trying to be a bigger person. "And you were born in the sky, I take it?"

Della watched her face, and Abby wondered if she had stepped over some invisible line. Then Della burst out laughing. "Pretty much!" Taking a glass from the busboy and drinking a quick swig, she beamed. "My mother was on trapeze with Ringling! She was the best of her day."

Abby didn't know what to say. This was clearly something Della hoped would impress her, but hadn't Della said her parents were on the vaudeville circuit when she was growing up? That her mother had had eight children? Still, Della was letting Abby use her tab and it seemed rude to question. Instead, she tried to come up with a reaction that Della would find suitable. "We went once, I think … in Chicago, but I was very little. It was impressive though."

"Still would have been before your time, probably. She died when I was tiny. Didn't exactly stick her landing, if you catch my drift."

This Abby found all the more jarring. She watched Della's face, trying to pinpoint what to say, but she found it hard to read. Her eyes were light, and her smirk challenging. It almost seemed as if she were using this story of her mother's death to shock Abby more than to relate to her. In an attempt to be sympathetic, Abby reached across the table to touch Della's arm, but she snatched it away.

"Look! The other girls got through!" She waved toward the door, where the group of three had just arrived. Abby recognized Vivian, but the other two looked quite different without their costumes and stage makeup. Trixie's hair was still red, but she had brushed out the tight ringlets, and without the heavy foundation and bright red rouge on her cheeks Abby could see the freckles that covered her face. The brunette's eyes appeared to have changed color now that they were no longer heavily lined and shadowed, and her brows had doubled in size.

"I've got to order them a round. It's tradition, 'cause I'm paid better. Excuse me." Della dashed toward the cluster at the door, leaving Abby nursing her drink alone.

The bar was definitely a dive, not even clean, but it seemed comfortable. She saw a few familiar faces from the carnival, but in general, it looked like the diner. The booths were the same mint-colored vinyl. The people wore the same circle skirts and brown slacks. It even had a large glass window at the front that captured the reflections of the patrons and made the room its own world, just like the diner at night. For the first time in two days, she felt safe and at ease with herself.

"Girls," Della began, leading the other three behind her like a chorus. "I want you to properly meet Abby Amaro."

"Amaro?" The brunette, her hair now tied up in a high ponytail with a yellow ribbon, asked. "That sounds really familiar."

Della sighed. "Yes, Celia, this is Natale's little sister."

The three girls all squealed. "Natale's so dreamy," said a voice from the group. It didn't belong to Celia, but Abby couldn't determine which one of them it came from. The girls seemed to have morphed into a single entity, and that was unsettling.

"I tried to hook him," Celia said conspiratorially, separating herself and dropping into the booth next to Abby. "But once his pretty brown eyes saw Della here spinning around like a madwoman, well, I didn't stand a chance."

The whole line of conversation made Abby uncomfortable. Natale was her brother. She knew that many girls found him attractive, but she had only twice seen him go on a date. "Maybe I should just go get another—"

"No!" cried Vivian, sliding into the seat across from Abby. "Stay. It's just us girls, and Celia's only trying to get a rise out of you."

"Am not."

Abby glanced at Della. A cloud seemed to have fallen over her face.

"Give us the real dish," demanded Trixie Rose. "When are we losing our Della? When are they tying the knot?"

Once again, Abby glanced at Della, searching for an answer. The cloud had turned to a full blown storm. Her jaw was clenched, and the look in her eyes was absolutely livid. Though Abby couldn't tell where it had come from, it seemed best to bow to it. She shook her head. "I don't … I'd never even heard of Della until yesterday."

"No?"

"No. Natale never—"

"That's it!" Della shouted. Her voice sounded strained, as if she were trying to be cheerful but wanted to rip the booth out of the wall at the same time. "Enough talk about me. Let's talk about Abby. She's got her own precious little love story, doesn't she?"

The trio leaned closer, and Abby wrapped her arms around herself as if trying to produce a protective barrier. "I'd really rather not talk about it."

"Oh, do," begged Celia.

"Yes, do," Della said, with a smirk.

"It doesn't actually have a happy ending."

"Well, that's a given," said Trixie Rose. "You wouldn't be here if it were a happy ending."

"You never know, Trix," said Della. "She could be in love with pin-faced Boleslaw."

"Della, don't be so mean," Vivian chastised.

"Viv is right," Celia said with a look of false reprimand. "If it's anyone, it's Marty, the human giant. They'd be cute! He's so tall. She's so short. They could do a double act!"

Opera rehearsals came rushing back to her: the soubrettes snickering behind their hands at her frizzy hair; the mutterings of "What does he see in her?" "Well, you know what they say about Italian girls." Abby shook her head. This was not the same. These girls were different. "We just don't get on anymore. It's no one here."

For a split second, the girls seemed saddened, until Trixie looked around with a conspiratorial smile and suggested, "We should set you up with someone, then."

"Yes, take your mind off all this sadness and woe," added Celia, wrapping her arm around Abby's shoulders and pulling her in. Her perfume was an acrid chemical approximation of oranges and roses.

Abby pulled back a little and looked over the girls, unsure of what to say. She had already met so many people in one day that any more would have completely overwhelmed her. "I'm not sure that I'm interested or ready yet."

The girls frowned once again.

"Well, then you need to get the emotions out. Tell us all about it," Vivian suggested. "Maybe I could turn it into a poem for you."

"No work at drinks!" Celia scolded.

"Or," Della said, raising her glass with a mocking smile, "Or you could sing about it. Didn't you say you were a singer?"

All color drained from Abby's face. "No, I don't ..." But Della was already climbing on the table and the other three were applauding.

"Everyone!" Della shouted, her voice carrying strongly over the din. As distracted as she was, Abby had to admit she was impressed. "Everyone, we've got a special treat for you. Straight from McClure's Traveling Amusements. A human canary!"

A few titters ran through the crowd as Della clambered down. Abby froze. She downed the rest of her cocktail, then began to sing the first aria that popped into her mind: the duke's song from *Rigoletto, La donna è mobile.*

Her voice cracked on the first notes and Della looked triumphant.

"Stand up," hissed Vivian from across the table. Abby obeyed. The sounds of the bar had died away. All faces were turned in Abby's direction. Her gut twisted, and she focused hard on a crack in the plaster in the opposite wall and tried to pretend she was alone, all alone, so no one else could hear her.

It didn't work. Her voice was too high. The key was wrong. Panic set in, and her notes began to sound flat. Her heart raced. She squeezed her eyes shut. When she opened them, she saw someone near the crack in the plaster. Abby averted her eyes, but they slowly drifted back to Suprema, who smiled and raised her glass. The gesture fortified Abby, and her heart slowed to its rightful pace.

When she reached a good stopping point in the song, she sat down. The bar patrons returned to their normal conversation, and the chorus girls applauded, this time quite sincerely. Della scowled, however, looking at her fellow performers as if they had committed a mutiny.

~May, 1957~

Frank's class ring, worn on a silver chain around Abby's neck, is cold and heavy on her skin. She lifts the ring lightly in her palm and examines it. The stone is a dark red garnet. Thinking about it makes Abby's laugh sound hollow and bitter. She hates to hear such a sound. The stone should have told Abby everything she needed to know about the man who gave her this ring. Frank was born in March; his birthstone is an aquamarine. He chose the garnet because the light blue stone struck him as "too girly." It was her birthday now, this still somewhat chilly-by-the-lake May day. Perhaps she should buy herself an emerald ring.

Briefly, Abby considers throwing the ring into the lake, where it would sink and join the rest of the things lost from time immemorial, vanishing forever, but she stops herself. She can't bear to part with it. Not yet. Not with the pain so fresh in her memory. She lets the ring drop from her palm and swing loosely on its chain as she walks.

"Abby!" a voice calls from behind her.

She doesn't stop. She knows who's following, though she's actually quite surprised. She didn't expect him to come after her. Not after what she saw.

"Abigail! Wait!"

Still, she keeps walking. The lakeshore is long. Of course, she knows the beach will end eventually, but by then, Frank will have long since stopped following.

"You know what, fine! Keep walking! No one wants to date an Italian girl who's been out in the sun anyway!"

She knows he wants to get a rise out of her and more than anything she wants to stop him from having what he wants. But she can't stop herself. She turns and faces him, trying hard to keep her eyes icy and hard though tears had been streaming from them just moments ago. She doesn't say a word. She crosses her arms and waits.

"You walk really fast when you're mad, you know that?"

Abby stares. His hair, a deep chestnut brown, is still in the same perfect ducktail he always wears. His eyes show no signs of tear tracks. He is not even out of breath. She regrets stopping. "What do you want, Frank?"

"To stop you from walking off with the wrong impression."

"Are you going to tell me it wasn't what it looked like? 'Cause your tongue was down her throat. I'm pretty sure it was exactly what it looked like."

"No. I'm not going to say that."

She has no idea how to respond. She looks away from him, out over the lake. She lets herself feel the cold air. It helps to numb the stinging at the corners of her eyes.

"You can still be my steady," Frank continues. 'This doesn't have to mean anything."

"You pushed me into a wall when Jimmy Correlli asked me to dance last week." She says the words matter-of-factly, as if it hadn't been one of the most terrifying nights she could remember. She had wanted to end it then, but Frank had seemed so contrite.

"That was different."

"Yes, Frank. Very different." She unclasps the silver chain, letting it and the garnet ring that should be aquamarine fall to the sand.

"Don't be such a wet rag," Frank calls after her as she turns to walk away again, slower this time, prouder, with fewer tears. "Who are you fooling, Amaro? No one else is ever going to want you."

He's said those words so many times. Too many parts of Abby believe them, but today she does not care if they are true. That is a problem for tomorrow. She walks toward the parking lot. She can catch a bus home from there.

"I loved you first!" Frank is still yelling, his voice harsh and aggressive, like tires on asphalt. "Remember that!"

She closes her eyes tight and tells herself to forget.

Chapter Eight

Nonna,

I don't know what Natale told you or the rest of the family, but I want you, out of everyone, to know my secret, especially because I am sure that the worst possibilities must be running through your mind. Nonna, I am traveling with a group of performers. Tonight we are leaving Toledo and heading into Michigan. I am so excited to see Detroit. I hear the opera there is first rate, as is most everything, or so they say.

I wish that you could see. Every night, they throw roses at my feet and call out for encores. It's everything you ever said it would be. Why just last night, we were performing a scene from Tosca, and I was asked to sing main soprano. As you know, this has never happened to me before, but you always said it would. Now it has!

Abby crumpled the letter, crushing it until her fingernails dug into her palm. Every word she had written was a lie, and she knew that Nonna Gaetana would see right through them. Still, she couldn't think of any way tell her how she was truly spending her days. She didn't know the words, in Italian or English, to write that for the past week, she had climbed onto a raised platform outside a tent and, in as commanding a voice as she could muster—which was unfortunately not all that commanding—cried out such nonsense as "Beyond this curtain you will find wonders that will never cease" and "Don't pass us by, you don't want to miss your one and only chance to see what lies in store" until her throat was hoarse. Instead of roses, people mostly threw contemptuous eye-rolls in her direction.

Some would be tempted enough to pay their quarter and pass into the tent, but even the nicest performers gave her sad, pitying expressions as if to say, "I don't want to complain, but you really aren't very good at this." No matter how many times Ruth and Constance said, "Don't worry. It's only your first week. You'll get the hang of it," Abby knew everyone was blaming her for their sudden drop in payouts. It had only taken two days before Boleslaw moved her from a platform in front of the sideshow to one in front of an exhibit tent full of rubber aliens and other fake "scientific artifacts."

"It's not that I don't trust you," he had said at the time, "it's just, these guys can sell themselves until you feel more comfortable."

With a sigh, she tossed the crumpled letter across the table.

They hadn't gone to Detroit, either, much to Abby's chagrin. She remembered her family discussing it a few years after her father came home from the war, just after Leon was born and they were still trying to figure out how to be a family again. Her mother had called it "The Paris of the West," and Abby had thought it would be paradise. Instead, though, the carnival had made camp outside a little town called Adrian, which was the furthest thing from Paris that Abby could imagine.

Della picked the crumpled letter up from the floor and squinted at its contents. "The only word I can read of this is Detroit. We never go to Detroit." She continued to stare hard at the words as if intense enough concentration could magically turn them into English. "I don't know why. Maybe their carnival market is too locked up at this time in the season. Adrian's not so bad, though. There's a real cute movie theater. Maybe we should check it out."

Eyebrows raised, Abby glanced at her. She seemed friendlier and more talkative than she had since their night out at the bar. "You seem cheery."

"Do I?" Della flattened Abby's letter on the edge of the table and handed it back to her. "Maybe it's because I just arranged a lovely dinner for two—"

"For your Adrian sweetheart?" Abby wasn't quite sure how to take this. Della had referred to Natale as her "Cleveland sweetheart" to his face; he had to know what was going on, and yet it felt like betraying her brother to encourage Della to spend time with other sweethearts.

"No, for you, silly."

Confusion growing with each passing moment, Abby stared at Della. "For me?"

"For you."

"With you?"

"Yes, a lovely romantic dinner with your brother's girl. No, I've set up a little candlelit spread with Vinnie." Her smile seemed almost mischievous. Warning bells went off in Abby's head.

"Vinnie who?"

"Just Vinnie. He's a sweetheart. Big personality. You'll love him."

Playful joy on her face, Della grinned and wiggled her eyebrows, but Abby didn't want to date anyone. She wanted to be left alone. "Do you really not even know his last name?"

"I've already handled everything," Della cooed, drifting behind Abby and twirling her dark brown curls between her fingers. Abby lifted her shoulders, trying to free her hair from Della's sudden grip. "You just need to show up at eight tonight. And look pretty. I can help with that, too."

"You better. You're the one who wouldn't let me pack."

Della blushed, and if Abby hadn't known it was an almost impossible thing to fake, she would have sworn it was for show. She was about to ask for more information about her blind date, but before she could get a word out, the loud slamming of trailer doors interrupted. Somewhere in the distance a great deal of shouting could be heard, but Abby couldn't make out the words.

Della froze like a rabbit that had heard a gunshot. "Get down," she hissed.

Abby stared. "What?"

"I said, get down."

Her expression brooked no argument, so Abby obeyed, slipping from her chair and sliding under the table. Della did the same. Edging under the side window so she couldn't be seen, she reached up and latched the door.

"What's going on?" Abby mouthed. The sounds of shouting and slamming doors were drawing closer.

Della shook her head. "Could be any number of things," she whispered.

Abby's head swam. It could be any number of things, and one of those things could be Frank. She hadn't expected him to try to track her down; he was a low-effort guy, but when his pride got involved, he could be unpredictable. His pride had definitely been involved. A few weeks into their relationship, he had thought a diner customer was flirting with her and broke his arm. This was worse. This was her rejection of him. Twice. In front of large groups of people.

It wasn't until Della put a hand on her arm to steady her that Abby realized she had been shaking the table. "Keep your head together," Della whispered, eyebrows raised.

Then came a knock on the trailer door. Abby stifled a scream. Della sucked in a breath, seeming to do the same.

"Open up!" a man's voice called, knocking again. "This is the police."

Della and Abby looked at each other, both silently deciding to stay quiet and not move.

The pounding continued.

"She's probably out," said the distinctly weighty voice of Boleslaw. There was a tone of authority in it that Abby hadn't heard before.

"Right," the policeman said in response. Abby could almost hear the sneer in his words. "Whose trailer is this then? You got a fat lady? Or something even more grotesque?"

In an instant, Della was on her feet and heading for the door. Abby dove to grab her by the ankle, but couldn't reach it in time. "I beg your pardon?" she asked, hip cocked to one side. Abby curled up tighter under the table. Terrible memories flashed through her brain, images of the men at her door when was just a little girl. "Who are you calling a grotesque?"

"And, what is your name, ma'am?"

"There's no shame in being a fat lady, you know," Della went on instead of giving her name. "She gets paid a wage just like the rest of us."

"So this show does have a fat lady?"

Boleslaw groaned.

"No," said Della. "But so what if we did? Is it a crime now to have put on a few pounds? Somebody better warn the candy butchers."

The officer hit the side of the trailer hard. The aluminum rattled, but Della didn't waver. "I'm just here to see to it that everything is up to code. And, I'll have you know, it is illegal in the state of Michigan for traveling shows to contain human monstrosities. It's not decent."

"Do I look like a monstrosity to you?" The words sounded like knives.

"I won't bother to ask if there's anyone else in there with you."

Della stepped aside and gestured grandly. "See for yourself." Abby cringed and pressed as far under the table as she could.

She had called his bluff. Somewhat deflated, the officer stepped out of the doorway and went on to the next trailer with Boleslaw following close behind.

Della ducked under the table and looked Abby in the eyes. "I won't bother to ask what that nonsense was about, but you *will* tell me later.

In the meantime …" She kicked open a small bottom panel that would have held a plumbing system if the trailer were ever parked at an actual campground with running water. "I need you to get to the Lambrinos's trailer and tell them to keep the ankle-biter safe. That one's got a look about him. He'll cart her right off if he lays eyes on her."

Abby shivered as the realization of what Della meant dawned on her. "But I don't know where—"

"The red double-decker with the orange awning at the far end. Farthest from action. There's always a mess of hula hoops and playing cards on the fold-out table next to it. Now go!" She shoved Abby out the plumbing hatch. "Hurry!"

Abby raced through the caravan, ducking in and out of rows of trucks and trailers, trying not to be seen. An angry crowd with Boleslaw at the head still followed the policeman. They provided enough distraction for Abby to get ahead of the group. She glanced back and caught Boleslaw's eyes. He gave an urgent nod, and she raced on even faster.

The Lambrinos's trailer was exactly as Della had described it, and Abby saw Ruth and Constance sitting at the table playing rummy.

"Gin!" Ruth cried, triumphantly laying out her cards.

Constance smiled, but a laugh died on her lips when she noticed an out-of-breath Abby. "Ruth," she hissed; Ruth turned, her eyes widening.

"Abby!" she exclaimed, rushing to help her to the table. "Are you all right? Can I get you anything?"

Abby shook her head. "No time," she forced herself to say. The words came with difficulty as she clutched the stitch in her side. "Police—tell you—Phebe."

Both girls jumped to action immediately. "I hate Michigan," Constance spat.

Ruth took her hand and squeezed it. "I'll take her. We'll just go collect flowers in the woods for a bit. She won't even know."

"She knows why this happens," Constance said with a frown, but she nodded and let go of Ruth's hand.

Ruth nodded in wordless understanding and hurried into the trailer to gather up Phebe. Abby waited with Constance and tried to stop her heart pounding as the noises of the crowd came closer.

"Does this happen often?" she asked.

Constance shrugged. "Depends on the town. Depends on the year. Depends on whether any crimes have been committed locally or if somebody's chickens got eaten by coyotes. We're easy scapegoats for all that. It's not as bad as it used to be, though. Least not how Papa tells it."

"My Nonna tells it the same."

The pair stayed silent, listening to the complaints and protests as they drew closer. Then Constance spoke again, her voice tense and stilted, but also urgent. "Why are you really here?" she probed.

"What?"

"I mean, you're not Della's sweetheart. I asked around."

Abby shook her head and felt a blush rise at the thought of Constance asking about her and Della in that way. "It's complicated."

"Are you hiding from someone?" Immediately, Abby understood the look in Constance's eyes. It wasn't a look meant for gossip; it was a sincere desire to help. Constance wanted to know if she should be in the woods with Ruth and Phebe. "If we need to hide you from them, I need to know now."

"I'm not what they're looking for today," Abby whispered. She wanted to hide, but for no reason other than the insistent pounding of her heart.

Constance gave a solemn nod. Abby had seen that expression before, on her grandmother, her mother, her father, Natale. It was a look of anxious resignation, the expectation that something was likely going to go wrong and that there was nothing to be done about it. Abby hated that expression.

The crowd turned the corner. Constance stood up; her expression hardened as if someone had just painted it with shellac. Though her entire body begged her to flee, Abby stayed right where she was, watching Constance's rigid face.

"This is the last trailer," Boleslaw said, gesturing toward the two of them. "As you can see ..."

The officer strode past him to Constance. With a look of annoyance at Boleslaw and the others who had followed him, he began speaking in a strained voice. "I am simply here to check that this organization is compliant with the local laws and that nothing untoward is being done here. I like to think that shouldn't be an inconvenience."

Constance locked her jaw before she spoke. Her words were slow, steady, and calm, but Abby could hear a venomous warning in them. "I'm sure you understand that people in our situation and line of employment can be sensitive about these matters."

"Because you have a reputation." He glanced at Abby, then back at Constance. "We've seen quite a few young women around and, to look at you—how can we be sure there isn't some sort of ... riding academy going on here?" Abby didn't understand the phrase, but she could tell from the smirk on the officer's face and the way Constance's fist clenched that it didn't have anything to do with horses.

Constance took a deep breath, releasing the tension in her hand. Abby was impressed. "I can assure you, sir, that all proper permits have been pulled, as I'm sure Mr. and Mrs. McClure, as well as Mr. Wolski, our lot manager, have already shown you and I'm sure countless others have already explained."

The look on his face was murderous. Constance's poise, unlike Della's, only seemed to aggravate him. "Gypsy trash," he muttered audibly.

"I'm sorry, sir, what was that?" Constance asked, not even blinking at the insult.

"You heard me," he said. He eyed the trailer, his eyes spinning over possible violations, but not settling on any one thing. "That's, uh, quite the trailer you've got there. I imagine a girl like you doesn't drive it herself. You got a husband? Kids? Other stowaways?"

"My father assists."

"You need that much space for you and an old—"

The trailer door flew open, interrupting. "Is there some kind of trouble out here?" Called a rail-thin man from the doorway. His accent had a dancing quality, making the words flow together almost like a song, but he looked groggy and half asleep.

"I got it under control, Papa," Constance said, her tone much sweeter now.

The officer spun away from her and started for the trailer. "Sir," he began. "Your 'daughter' here was just informing me that you and she alone occupy this massive trailer."

Constance's father nodded. "That is correct. We make a fair wage. Our skills are unique and in demand."

The officer smirked, taking in Mr. Lambrinos's haggard looks. "Skills like opium dealing? Or maybe you're spies?"

His eyes narrowed. "We had a long drive last night and only finished setup a few hours ago. You would begrudge a man a nap?"

"What is your name, sir?"

"Alejo Lambrinos. And what is yours?"

The people gathered around Boleslaw were hushed. They barely seemed to breathe. Abby was terrified that the officer would take Constance's father, and possibly Constance herself, away in handcuffs. And what would she tell Ruth?

Just as the officer seemed ready to move forward, Boleslaw intercepted him. "Sir, as you can see, we are a plenty tame group of nomads. How about you step off to my tent and I'll get you a hot coffee."

Still Abby could not breathe.

He paused, watching Boleslaw with piercing eyes. He glanced toward the crowd and, in an instant, deflated. "I'd prefer lemonade."

"I think that could be arranged." Boleslaw wrapped an arm around the officer's shoulders and, with a wink back at Abby and Constance, led him away and through the crowd.

As soon as he was gone, Constance let out a long slow breath. "I'll go get Ruth and Phebe," she said.

Abby stood up to follow, but thought better of it. She stayed in place, watching Constance go. Her stride was confident and determined even after the demeaning confrontation. A small worm of envy climbed through Abby's gut. She had been terrified. She didn't know if she could move at all.

"Were you afraid, Miss?" Constance's father asked.

Abby nodded, still not sure if she could speak.

"Oh, don't you worry. Boleslaw is the best lot manager we've ever had. He'd never let anything happen to any of us. I've known him for many years."

Again, Abby nodded. She was glad Mr. Lambrinos had that trust, but wasn't quite sure that she shared it.

Chapter Nine

THE RESTAURANT HAD A NICE look about it. It wasn't the Ritz by any means, but it was clean and hardly the dive Abby had expected Della to have chosen. In fact, though she was trying hard not to think about Cleveland, the facade made her mind drift back to the diner. It was Wednesday night. Back home, the special would be chopped sirloin with stuffed tomatoes. The milkshake flavor of the day would be chocolate, unless Sal got it in his head to be fancy, in which case he would show up with a crate of pineapples and spend half the night trying to cut them up fast enough for excited Coventry teens until Roman gave up and opened the canned pineapple that had been hidden away for the next day's ham steaks.

Thinking of Sal and Roman brought another memory: the top-hatted ride jockey she had met on her first day at the carnival. He had been swept from her mind until this very moment, lost in the excitement, confusion, and anxiety of the days that followed. She wracked her brain trying to remember his name. Perhaps he could be Vinnie? She had been too preoccupied to feel any attraction to him, but he had been nice, friendly, and kind. If she was going to be set up with one of the carnival folk, well, she figured that she could do worse.

She adjusted the far-too-tight yellow bell dress that Della had insisted she wear and pushed open the door. Immediately an eager hostess stepped toward her. The restaurant looked practically deserted; Abby knew well how bored she must be. "Slow night?" she asked, as if talking to a coworker.

The hostess nodded enthusiastically. Abby watched her face. Her eyes had a hopeful quality that offset the weariness the heavy bags under them suggested. "Wednesday's not a big night for us. Chicken liver special."

Abby laughed. "I actually like chicken livers, believe it or not. I'll have to buy out your supply."

The hostess beamed. "Chicken liver table for one?"

Abby was about to agree. It would be the first decent meal she'd had in longer than she wanted to admit. Did she really want to be forced to share it with a stranger? Still, it was rude to bail on a date, and it made the other person involved feel terrible. She should know; Frank had bailed on her often enough. "Actually, I'm meeting someone. Ah, Vinnie … something."

Her eyes narrowing a little, the hostess peered at her list. After a long moment, she pressed her lips together and nodded. "Right. This way, please." She led Abby toward the back. In a fancier restaurant in a larger town, Abby might have assumed the location was meant to provide privacy, but she knew enough about the restaurant business to know that a table hidden behind a small wall near the kitchen meant something quite different in a place like this.

Seated at the table with a half-finished glass of beer in front of him was an older, balding gentleman wearing a shabby suit. He stood as they approached. "You must be Abby," he said, extending a hand.

Abby wanted to recoil. She looked to the hostess for assistance, but she was already hurrying back to the lobby. Abby simply nodded, not shaking his hand. "And you're Vincent?"

He sat and took a swig of his beer. "I am. I'm the poor old drunk Della Adamson and her posse like to set up on dates with new girls to embarrass them. Don't worry; you're not the first one they've done this to and you won't be the last."

Abby stared hard at him. She was angry. This whole blind date nonsense had been done to embarrass her? So much for new friends. They were exactly like the girls at the opera. She didn't know why she had expected anything else.

"Excuse me," Abby said, trying to maintain her composure. "I have to go."

"Sit," Vinnie said, still sounding a little bitter, but somewhat more cordial. "Pick out the most expensive bottle of wine they've got and whatever you want for dinner."

"I couldn't possibly—"

"I know this isn't a real date," he said and gave a hearty laugh. "And don't worry; you're not even close to my type. But Adamson gives me the money for this nonsense, so seriously, if you want to get back at her, go to town. Order expensive things."

Still, Abby stayed on her feet. "Why are you here if you knew what they're up to?"

"You really want to eat either concessions or the slop they try to pass off in the food tent every night?"

It didn't take any more convincing. She sat and took the wine list in hand. "I don't care if French wine is more expensive. Can we get something Italian? I'm feeling a little homesick."

Vinnie's eyes lit up. *"È così?"*

Abby bit her lip. She knew what Vinnie was thinking. Whenever she talked about her family or spoke Italian, people assumed that, rather than being the child of immigrants, she herself was from Italy. "I mean ..."

"Che città?"

"I, uh, Palermo?" She shifted in her chair and looked to the floor. Now she'd done it. This had happened a few times when she worked at the diner. Less and less these days, of course, as Italy was gradually morphing into a place that people in Abby's world visited rather than a place that they were from. Still, every time, she was struck with the sensation that she was an imposter, claiming something that she, herself, didn't actually have any right to own, and yet it was still part of her.

"No need to be ashamed. It's too beautiful a home to be ashamed of. In fact, I would have kicked you out of my table if you had said anywhere north of Naples."

"No, I'm not ashamed. I just don't want you to misunderstand. I've never … actually been there, myself, you know," Abby explained. "My parents were younger than I am now when …"

Vinnie nodded and waved a hand, attempting to summon a waiter. At first they seemed to ignore him, but, after a moment, one took their order. "So you've never been home?"

"My home is Cleveland," Abby explained. "I was born there." She examined Vinnie's face. It was a brilliant red color, as if he spent hours a day scrubbing his skin. She wondered what his act might be that would require that.

"Cleveland," Vinnie muttered, a hint of distaste in his voice. "I remember Cleveland. Whyever would you leave?"

An unexpected feeling of protectiveness rushed through her. Hearing a stranger imply that there was something wrong with the place she grew up, the place her family lived, perfect or not, hurt. "I didn't really have a choice," she snapped. "I wouldn't have gone if I did."

With a bemused smirk, Vinnie took another sip of beer. He didn't seem convinced. "I've been with McClure's Amusements for almost ten years. Never seen 'em force anybody to join the caravan. Doubt they'll start anytime soon."

"You know what I mean."

"You mean you have a sob story?" Vinnie asked. "We all do. Doesn't mean it's not a choice."

Abby pondered this. Part of her still wanted to punch him, but another appreciated his frankness.

"That's the trouble with you kids," he continued. "You're all convinced that no one else has ever struggled like you do."

"You have a sob story then?" she challenged.

"Of course I do. I'm a clown. Our stories are the saddest of all."

Abby fought back a laugh, unsure whether or not he had meant to be amusing. At least being a clown explained the overly-scrubbed state of his face. She took a deep breath and attempted to arrange her features into a look of sincerity. "Would you tell me?"

Vinnie seemed skeptical, almost as if he could read the laugh still hiding in Abby's eyes, but then he nodded. "We've got to stick together, don't we?"

Abby didn't know what to say. She waited patiently as her wine was poured. After a few more sips of his beer, Vinnie began. He told her a long and detailed tale about running away from his home in Salerno to New York when he was just a teenager and how hard travel had been just after the first World War; about becoming an autoworker in Detroit, then becoming a hobo after the drink caught up with him; about joining up with the carnival; and finally, after he had almost finished another glass of beer, about why he had run away in the first place: the love of his life, a young man named Gianni.

"We were supposed to run together, you know. Both of us. He never showed. Then, a couple months later, I get a little note from his sister—he was dead. I took it harder than I like to admit."

Abby stared blankly at his face, unsure of what to say.

"What, do I shock you?" Vinnie asked. "Completely disturbed by the degenerate clown?"

"No," said Abby immediately. "It's just—I can't imagine."

She had never felt that desperate love that would be strong enough to carry you away from everything you'd ever known. Not for Frank. Not for anyone. She was running *from* Frank. That was quite different.

"What was Gianni like? Do you still ...?"

"Think about him every day." Vinnie smiled wistfully into the amber liquid in his glass, and Abby knew he wasn't seeing his own reflection there.

VINNIE WALKED ABBY BACK TO Della's trailer around ten. The lights were on inside. She sighed. "I was hoping she'd still be out."

"Adamson is harmless," Vinnie whispered. Abby thought his hushed tones contradicted this statement, but said nothing. "She's a sad, lonely little girl who misses a mother who died too young, just like you."

"But I never said—"

"No need." Vinnie took her hand and squeezed it. "I can read people better than they think I can. Now, Miss Amaro. This has been a lovely evening. I appreciate that you didn't run screaming. I might have, in your shoes."

Abby shook her head. "No. This was fun. I haven't had Chianti in forever."

Vinnie kissed her hand. "Goodnight, Miss Amaro."

He disappeared into the darkened trailer lot, and Abby watched as he left. She couldn't imagine her own life playing out as his had, and yet there was something about him, something sweet and kind. Could she be sweet and kind after losing someone who meant that much to her? Would anyone ever mean that much to her?

Della's trailer door creaked open, spilling light out into the lot. "Abby? Is that you? Are you home?" Della called out into the darkness. Abby took that as her cue to hurry up and get inside. There she found Trixie Rose, Vivian, and Celia all crammed around the tiny table. They looked up at her expectantly.

"How was your date?" Della asked, a smirk dancing on her lips as she latched the door behind Abby. An amused giggle rippled through the other three.

Abby stared at the three other girls and then looked back at Della. Their eyes were all trained on her, waiting for her to get mad and yell at Della, or cry, or something. Abby simply shook her head and went to the bench Della had made up for her bed. Abby curled up and turned to face the wall, though she knew she wouldn't be able to sleep. She was sick to her stomach and certain it had nothing to do with the chicken livers or the wine.

"Come on, don't be like that. It's just a little hazing," Celia said, her inflection rising at the ends of her sentences. When Abby didn't answer, she turned to Della with the same tone. "Della..."

Della stayed quiet, though Abby listened hard to hear her response. She could hear her heels click against the linoleum as she paced and the rustle of fabric, as if she were rummaging through it or pinning something new to her dummy, which usually seemed to soothe her.

After a long while she sighed. "You guys should go."

"Del—" Vivian began, but Della cut her off.

"Nah, she's sleeping, and it's late. I've got some letters to write anyway."

"If you're sure." Skirts shuffled and heels clicked as the girls went out into the trailer lot.

"I know you're awake," Della said when they'd gone.

Abby still didn't answer her.

"It was just supposed to be a joke."

"I get that," Abby answered, still not turning to face her. She couldn't distill what she was feeling into words for Della.

"Are you really that mad?"

"No," Abby answered, sitting up. "I'm not mad. I just... How much do you know about Vinnie?"

Della shrugged. "He's a clown. He'll put up with a lot of nonsense if you offer to pay for his dinner. Why? Did he get fresh with you? He's never—"

"We just had a nice talk."

"Hmm," was Della's only response. She went back to her dress dummy and fluffed the skirt.

Abby frowned and attempted another tactic. "You love my brother, right?"

Della fluffed the skirt again and did not answer.

"Okay. Goodnight then," Abby said, lying back down. She closed her eyes and listened a little while longer to Della fidgeting with the clothes on the dress dummy.

~June, 1957~

ABBY STARES UP AT THE darkened house on Murray Hill Road. Exactly one hour and twenty-three minutes have passed since her curfew, and not a single light has been turned on. She knows because she has been waiting.

In the driver's seat next to her, Marjorie lights another cigarette. "If you don't want to go in, we can drive around a little more," she suggests after taking a drag.

Abby smiles. Nothing appeals to her more than driving away from the house, with Marjorie's brand new FM radio blaring whatever WHK chooses to play. She reaches out and turns up the volume. Elvis croons, and Abby laughs. "Just drive."

Marjorie flicks cigarette ash out the window, then glances over at Abby. One eyebrow is cocked. "You sure?"

"Miles from here. Far away. Just keep driving and don't stop."

Marjorie laughs nervously. "We could go to New York."

Excited that she is playing along, Abby grabs her free hand and grins. "Yes! New York! Wouldn't that be wonderful?"

"Yeah." Marjorie's tone is wistful and Abby actually thinks that a plan might be unfolding. "We could get an apartment in the village. I could sell my paintings—" Then the dreamy smile that has formed on her pale pink lips fades. "What about the opera?"

"New York has great opera," Abby says, not willing to give up on the rush of freedom just yet.

"But you're in school for opera here." She takes one last long drag off the cigarette and tosses it out the window. "Besides, I don't have the gas money to drive that far."

Abby deflates as Elvis sings "uh huh" one last time. A light comes on in the house, and Abby sighs. "And, there's my cue."

"Sorry. Maybe we'll go to New York next weekend?" Marjorie teases.

"Sure," Abby smiles and slips out of the car. The light looks like it's coming from Nonna Gaetana's window, which is unlucky. Abby has to pass that room to get to her own. She swallows hard and glances back at Marjorie, who gestures toward the house encouragingly before starting her car. Abby frowns as Marjorie's car pulls away, then, silently hoping that her grandmother merely needs a drink of water and will be back to sleep before Abby turns the corner, steels herself to make her way through the mostly darkened house.

No such luck.

When Abby turns down the hallway toward her room, she sees that Nonna Gaetana's door is ajar. She is waiting. Beneath Abby's feet, a floorboard creaks, sealing her fate.

"Abigaille?" her grandmother's voice calls from her room.

Abby sucks in a deep breath and holds it, not daring to move even an inch.

"Abigaille, I know you're out there."

Ever so slowly, she lets out the breath and slips into her grandmother's room. Nonna Gaetana sits on her bed, clutching an envelope full of pictures. She does not look at the pictures, but Abby knows what is to come. This has happened before. "Nonna," Abby says softly, going to her side. "Nonna, it's late. You should get back to sleep. You need your rest."

Nonna shakes her head. "I'm not tired."

Abby knows better than to argue. Instead, she nods, accepting that it may be a long night. "Would you like to tell me about the people in the pictures, Nonna?"

"Pictures?"

Gingerly, Abby touches the hand holding the envelope. The hand is delicate and thin, and Abby does not like to touch it because she is reminded of how fragile her grandmother's health has been of late.

"Oh," Nonna Gaetana says, her eyes resting on the envelope. "No, we've talked about them plenty of times, haven't we?"

They have. Many, many times. Always as if it were the first time. "Yes, Nonna," Abby admits, not sure what this change means. "I thought it helped you get to sleep."

"Not tonight."

"All right." Abby stays silent, waiting. The stillness is too heavy, like dead air on the radio. She expects words, but none come. She fidgets, rubbing at a hand with her thumb.

"Where were you tonight?" Nonna Gaetana finally asks.

Abby finds it easier to answer this question now that she is no longer going steady with Frank. "Went to a drive-in with Marjorie. There's a new Cary Grant movie out."

"Marjorie…"

"From the diner," Abby explains patiently. Her grandmother has been apt to forget names lately.

"I know who Marjorie is," Nonna Gaetana protests. "You talk about her all the time lately."

Abby blushes.

"You two have been spending an awful lot of time together."

Her grandmother's critical tone takes Abby by surprise. It is a few moments before she can defend herself. "We… work together, Nonna. At the Cedar Road Diner. Remember?"

"Don't you talk to me as if I'm going senile, Abigaille Giovanna Amaro. I see more than you children realize."

"Nonna..."

"You need to spend less time with that girl. If you go to drive-ins, go in a group like Natale does. He is a sensible boy."

"Nonna, I don't understand what you're talking about!" She is shouting. She hates shouting at her grandmother. She scolds Natale for doing it, for being impatient when Nonna can't remember things or tells the same story twice, but this is different. Her grandmother is angry with her, but she can't wrap her mind around why. "Are you all right?"

Nonna Gaetana stares at Abby's face. "How old are you? You should get married. That is what girls your age are supposed to do."

"Nonna!"

"Whatever happened to the Butler boy?"

Abby grimaces. "We split up," she says as quickly as possible. It's the best way to pull off the Band-Aid.

Nonna Gaetana says nothing. Then she stands and looks at Abby, holding out her hands. "Why would you do something like that?"

Abby takes her hands and attempts to gently steer her back to sitting. She doesn't want to hurt her grandmother, who is suddenly stronger than she remembers, but she is confused. She lets Nonna Gaetana pull away and pace over to the writing desk. She stands and takes tentative steps toward her. "I thought you didn't like him? You complained all the time that he wasn't Italian, that he didn't have a real job, that he was lazy and pompous—"

"By the time I was your age, I was married with a baby on the way."

"I don't want to marry Frank!" Abby insists. She wants to run away, to slam the door on her grandmother and shut out this conversation. "He cheated on me! He hurt me!"

Nonna Gaetana waves a hand as if swatting away a fly. "That's men. Good girls still marry them."

Abby shakes her head and starts for the door. There is no more she can do. "I can't accept that, Nonna, I'm sorry."

Nonna Gaetana presses her face to her hands as if praying. Abby closes the door behind her as quietly as she can.

Chapter Ten

As setup began in Kalamazoo, Abby sat on the step outside Della's trailer, waiting for the advance man to bring the mailbag. She was supposed to be trying to mend several burst seams in Della's costumes, but she had already stabbed her finger with the needle four times in the past ten minutes. Her mind was elsewhere. She was desperately searching the crowds of people slipping in and out of the trailer lot for any sign of Natale. He'd said he'd pick her up in Kalamazoo or Chicago. That had been weeks ago, but it was the only thing she had to go on as she hadn't heard from him since.

When the mail finally came around, Abby called out, but Thomas frowned and shook his head, passing her by. Not even a letter from one of Della's admirers. Her heart sank. Seconds later, anger had replaced despair. Her brain whirled through a myriad of un-Natale-like actions. Had her brother forgotten about her? Did he have better things to do? Abandoning her never seemed like something he would do, but neither did dating a girl like Della. Incensed, she stood and, Della's costumes still clenched in her fist, marched off in search of a pay phone.

She found one near the front of the lot. Under normal circumstances, she would have been embarrassed to have this conversation in front of so many people, but setup kept them distracted and anger pushed away any thought of embarrassment.

She tried the Amaro house twice, but there was no answer. Panic rising in her chest, she dialed the only other number she could think of: the diner. The phone rang four times before she heard Sal's voice, "Cedar Road Diner. Our hours are—"

"Sal!" Abby hissed into the phone, keeping her voice low for reasons she didn't fully understand.

"Abby?! Is that you?"

"Yes, Sal." She glanced around nervously, but no one, not even the crew, appeared able to hear. "It's me."

"Where are you? Where have you been?" His voice sounded frantic.

"It's complicated, Sal. Natale—"

"Fed us all some line about you being sick, but when Roman went to take you some soup, he got all cagey about how contagious you were, and no one was allowed in."

"Oh, well …" Abby faked a cough. "That is—"

"Bullshit, is what it is. We asked Leon, and he was pretty clear about the fact that no one in your whole family has seen you in over a month. A month, Abby!"

"I know how long it's been, Sal."

"Then where are you? What's going on?"

"I'll explain everything when I get back. It's just … have you seen Natale? Recently, I mean?"

"Abby—"

"What about my dad? The kids? You said you'd talked to Leon—"

"Like a week ago, Abby. And those circumstances—"

"What circumstances? You haven't seen them?"

"It's not that. How about you just tell me what's going on?"

"What about Frank? Have you seen him? Has he been in the diner?"

"Abby!" Sal shouted, sounding confused and frustrated. "Don't flip your wig. Just tell me what's happening. Are you in trouble? Are you hurt?"

Abby took a deep breath, trying to calm her racing mind. "I just want to know if everyone's okay."

"I need to know if you're okay first."

She didn't like the word "first" at the end of that sentence. Her brain was already concocting a million terrible scenarios for why Sal needed her to be "okay first" before he told her about her family. Her father had lost his job. They had lost their house. The house had been set on fire. One of her siblings had been hurt. Killed. Suddenly, she gasped and slammed down the receiver. Telling herself that she would apologize to Sal later, she forced herself to breathe. Unable to bring in a full breath, she turned and rested her back against the pay phone.

The temp workers Della called roughies were continuing their setup, directed by Boleslaw and a few other men Abby didn't know. They were oblivious to her presence. Abby had seen setup a few times now, and it was beginning to lose whatever novelty it had once held. This time, however, something about the setup ritual seemed strange. Their faces, even those of the men drafted from the townies who hung around setup, men she had definitely never seen before, looked oddly familiar. She stared, trying to determine the source of this familiarity, but it was hard to get a good look at anyone. They moved swiftly, too swiftly, almost as if they were shadows, shadows with a very particular face: Frank Butler's face. Logically, she knew it was impossible for each one of these men to be Frank, but she still felt herself seize up with terror that seemed to descend from her head down through her whole body. When it reached her feet, all logical thought vanished, and she ran blindly through the booths and tents, ducking and swerving until she reached the trailers.

She wasn't looking for Della. Della would perhaps understand, but she would certainly make a joke or two and then send her back out for one reason or another. The Lambrinos family, however, they would let her hide out for a while. In her panicked state, she couldn't remember any distinguishing characteristics of their trailer. Seeing a hula hoop resting outside a door, she threw it open and rushed inside, hoping she'd chosen correctly.

She hadn't. For starters, the trailer was much smaller; smaller even than Della's. Where the Lambrinos's trailer had separate sleeping areas and even a living room of its own, this trailer could barely house a table. On that table, the radio hummed away. Whatever station it had been tuned to, though, had devolved into static. Behind a curtain to the left, someone stirred. Ever so slowly, Abby backed up, inching toward the door, when suddenly the curtain was pulled back to reveal Suprema. Abby stopped moving, transfixed partially by fear and partially by the sight of Suprema's mahogany hair. Much longer than Abby had realized, it had been loosed from its elaborate bun and tousled by sleep. A strange buzzing started in the back of her mind. She couldn't pinpoint its origin or why it had begun, but she knew that was the loveliest hair she had ever seen. She couldn't move an inch. She could only stare.

Suprema stared back. "What are you doing here?" she asked after a long, tense moment.

Abby didn't remember how to form words. She stayed silent, forcing her brain to comb through the last several minutes and drag out whatever it could come up with. "I just … got lost … I guess," she finally said after a great deal of mental effort.

Suprema cocked her head and continued to stare, the confusion on her face seeming to grow with each passing second. "Lost? What were you looking for?"

The words still weren't coming, and the buzz was far too loud. Abby felt as if she were taking an oral exam and hadn't studied for it. "Well, I …" she began before trailing off, unable to come up with an explanation that didn't make her sound as though she had lost her mind.

This lack of explanation was obviously not good enough for Suprema, who was on her feet in an instant. "Della Adamson sent you in here, I suppose. One of her first-of-May hazing rituals?"

"No. I'm sorry. I didn't mean to disturb you—" Abby took a few steps back toward the door and fumbled for the handle.

Instead of chasing her out, as Abby had expected, Suprema began to pace. She could only move a few steps in each direction, but judging from the worn vinyl flooring in that spot, she did this often. "Little Precious thinks she's so special. But you know, you don't have to do what she says. You don't have to be part of her club. She's a total Veronica, and Vinnie says you're nice, you don't need to be around a Veronica—"

"There was a hula hoop," Abby said meekly.

Suprema looked at her more closely. "What?"

"There was a hula hoop," Abby repeated. "I was looking for Constance and I wasn't thinking straight. I… I guess."

As she uncrossed her arms, Suprema seemed to soften. "You don't have to cry. Please don't cry."

Abby hadn't realized that she had been crying, but now that Suprema mentioned it, she felt the tears of fear, concern, frustration, and embarrassment. "I—"

Suprema walked toward Abby. Her moves were slow and deliberate, as if she were approaching a feral cat she thought would bolt. "How about we try this again? Quieter this time. Why are you in my trailer?"

A voice in the back of Abby's mind told her to flee, but almost immediately another voice, one that was intrigued by the never-before-seen look of gentleness in Suprema's eyes, told her to stay put. "I really was looking for Constance or Ruth. I just wanted to sit in their trailer for a while until I felt better."

"But the Lambrinos's trailer—"

"I know," Abby admitted, looking down at the floor. "I saw a hula hoop outside and my mind just, misinterpreted, I guess. Sometimes, it gets a little … especially lately," she trailed off again, allowing Suprema to help her to a chair.

"Did someone hurt you?" Suprema asked, her voice slow and patient.

Abby shook her head, her cheeks hot. "Not anytime recently."

"However recent it was doesn't matter." Suprema took one of her hands. The gesture was comforting.

The pair sat in silence for a long while, until Suprema spoke again. "I'm sorry I yelled at you. I was worried, because you're friends with Della—"

"Della's not really my—" but Abby stopped herself from finishing that sentence. In many ways Della had been a friend to her—not a great one, but she tried. "Della's just looking after me for a while. Until it's safe."

A light of understanding seemed to dawn behind Suprema's eyes, as if she were putting together the pieces of a mystery that had been baffling her. "You're the girl from the Cleveland show!" she exclaimed, jumping to her feet. "I thought you looked familiar somehow, but I couldn't place it. Not quite, but … you are, aren't you?"

Abby didn't want to nod, but she did.

"It was that man, wasn't it? The one who interrupted? He's the one who hurt you?"

Again, Abby nodded, though she didn't want to.

"I'm so sorry."

"It wasn't your fault."

Suprema went to a cupboard and pulled out a small cooler, from which she produced two bottles of soda. She handed one to Abby. "It might be a little warm, but I try to keep a stash in here, since my uncle isn't too fond of me begging off the vendors."

Abby looked around for a bottle opener, but Suprema took back the bottle and popped the top off on the edge of the table. Abby looked on, impressed. "I forget that it's not a trick."

Not acknowledging this, Suprema took the top off her bottle and sipped her soda. "You don't have to tell me anything you don't want to, you know. I know I don't exactly … engender trust and openness."

Abby sipped, watching Suprema. She did trust her, somehow. They hadn't had a single civil conversation before today, and yet Abby had warmed to her, as though she were the only person who could truly understand. After another sip of her soda, Abby explained who Frank was and why he had done what he did that night, as well as the terrifying aftermath. She told Suprema how she hadn't heard a word from her family, and how Sal had been so evasive about the state of them; how the faces of the roustabouts had seemed to transform before her eyes. She expected Suprema to look shocked or confused, but instead she nodded slowly.

"He doesn't sound like a very good person," she whispered when Abby had finished speaking.

"No. I learned that," Abby said.

"I'm glad you were able to break away." A silence hung between them. Suprema gingerly held onto Abby's hand. Though she didn't understand why, Abby felt solid ground beneath her feet for the first time since she'd left home.

After a long while, Suprema stood with a sigh. She picked up the empty soda bottles and looked at Abby. "You know, if you ever need to, for any reason, ever again, you're welcome in my trailer anytime."

This, Abby had not been expecting. She stared unblinking until she managed to force out, "I couldn't impose."

Suprema shook her head. "Nothing of the sort. Vinnie said you were nice, and … well, I've heard you sing. Anyone who sings like that can't be that bad."

Abby ducked out of Suprema's trailer with her heart pounding and her head still buzzing. The buzz wasn't unpleasant. In fact, it felt nice. Still, she wasn't sure what to make of it. She wasn't sure what to make of any of it. She barely had the chance to try. Just a few steps out the door, she walked right into Boleslaw.

“I’m sorry, Miss Amaro,” he said, backing away. His face was shiny, covered in a thick layer of petroleum jelly. Abby was impressed by what he put himself through for his art.

“No, I—”

“I was seeking my niece.” He glanced at Suprema’s trailer. “Is she awake?”

Abby nodded. She still couldn’t figure out what to make of her exchange with Suprema. She stepped aside and started away.

“Miss Amaro,” Boleslaw said, reaching for the trailer door and stopping mid-knock, “I must admit I’m surprised to see you here at all. Miss Adamson said that you would probably only be with us until our arrival here in Kalamazoo.”

“She wasn’t wrong at the time,” Abby said, trying to sound as cordial as possible. Part of her wanted to start running blindly again, but Boleslaw was blocking the doorway to the place her feet were telling her to go.

“There’s been a change of plans?”

“It would seem so.”

Boleslaw nodded and reached into his pocket. He pulled out a small card and handed it to Abby. On it was printed a list of cities and dates. She scanned the places and sure enough, “Kalamazoo, Michigan, August 17-26, PO BOX M-136.” was printed on it. It was more than halfway down. From there the troupe continued west to Chicago, then looped back down around through southern Ohio before reaching their last destination of “Lexington, Kentucky, PO BOX M-2038” in mid-October.

“It’s a route card,” Boleslaw explained. “In case you decide not to stick around and need to let someone know how to find you.”

Abby held it as reverently as she would have held a prayer card, which was about the same size and shape. There might still be a way home after all. “Thank you,” she whispered.

Boleslaw nodded a "don't mention it," then knocked on Suprema's trailer door. Abby made herself scarce before any sort of argument began.

~April, 1956~

Calvary Cemetery is farther out of the city than Abby would like. Lakeview was beautiful and just down the street, but of course her mother couldn't be buried there. No matter the distance, she visits her mother as often as she is able, but she's the only one who does. It strikes her as odd, considering that the entire family used to picnic at the family plot when she was a little girl. At least once a month, the whole Amaro clan would pack a basket and go have lunch with Nonno and Zio Francesco, for whom they left all the burnt biscotti, and she would walk among the stones, noting the names and dates with a quiet curiosity. Abby never realized that not everyone did this until, over time, everyone else stops coming, and it is just Abby, staring at only one name: Ninfa Amaro.

"I think you'd be proud, Mama," she whispers to the stone in front of her. "I got into the Institute of Music's opera program. I only went flat two times in the audition. I was shocked, honestly. I thought I did much worse."

Her words drift off into silence. The silence is the hardest part. She thinks that's why no one else visits. Ninfa Amaro used to be full of things to say, full of music and life, always singing folk songs, but now she is silent. Abby tries to fill in her side of the conversation in her mind, but comes up blank.

"I've already been to two classes," she rambles on, unable to bear the silence any longer. "It's hard. You know I've never been very good in front of people. It makes me, what was it you always said, wobbly? It makes me wobbly."

She waits. No answer comes; not that she expects one. Still, her mother would have said it was rude to ramble on without stopping to let the other person talk. The air is warming up. It has been a long winter, made longer by yet another year without Mama's canned tomato sauces and pickled peppers, without Mama's Easter bread. Now spring has arrived and there are fewer things to go without. For now.

"The teachers are nice," Abby says after pausing to mentally fill in what her mother would say at this point about poise and confidence. "The other students, not so much, but I just don't know them yet, I think. Maybe after a little while, they'll let me into their little clubs."

The waiting is too much. Abby sighs and gets to her feet. Exhaling slowly, she drops a drawing of Joseph's and a little packet of fennel seeds she had been saving. She knows deep down that she might not come back again. No one else does, and now she remembers why. She hates the silence.

Chapter Eleven

Natale,

Had I written this letter a day ago, it would have been a rather angry one. I have been wondering why I haven't heard a word from you since I left and yesterday I got it into my head that you had decided not to come and get me after all. That's not the case, is it?

How is everyone at home? I miss you all and can't help but worry over your well-being. I don't even know what Dad said when he saw your face. Or what Leon said! I imagine he was awestruck. How are Carla and Annette? Carla's been so taciturn lately. You would think she was the one was about to turn thirteen and not Leon. There is a little girl here who reminds me of the two of them if you rolled them up into one person and added a little of Joseph's insecurities. What I'm trying to say is I miss all of you. And Dad. And Nonna. All of you.

I have copied out our route card on the back of this note in case you don't have one and that is why I haven't heard from you. The PO box number is different for most of the towns, which I hope explains the lack of contact.

Please write soon, Natale. Your sister misses you.

Love,
Abby

"Today only! See the amazing discovery! Two mummified alien bodies on loan from New Mexico!" Abby called out to the crowd. Occasionally one or two of the people trailing through would peer over in her direction. Even less occasionally, a teenager would drift away from their family, turn their face toward Abby and hold out a hesitant quarter. More often than not, their parents would notice and pull them away before Abby could collect.

The sun blazed down, scorching everything, especially Abby's bally platform. She wanted more than anything to make a mad dash for the lemonade stand, and part of her was tempted to do it. The exhibit would have just as much luck selling tickets without her.

"Anything?" Ruth asked as she walked over to the platform with her box of lunches, looking up at Abby with a concerned expression. Abby knew that expression. She knew everything about that expression, even if she didn't know all that much about Ruth. It was an expression she had seen countless times before on her teachers' faces. It said, "I know you're trying so hard and I don't want to tell you what I'm really thinking about your performance, but it's substandard."

Abby swallowed hard. It was one thing to see her teachers looking that way and another to see it in a friend. "This is getting ridiculous," she muttered, trying to keep her tone light.

"The aliens aren't working?" Ruth asked, sounding shocked. "People love aliens."

"I've had maybe two kids try to come in—" As she said this, a gaggle of teenagers walked by and Abby called out to them. One of the boys elbowed another in the ribs, but he shrugged and the group walked on. "I don't know what I'm doing wrong. They're all like that."

Ruth pressed her lips together. "Let me give it a try."

Without a second thought, Abby stepped to the side. "Platform's all yours."

"Ladies and Gentlemen!" Ruth called as she climbed onto the platform. Her voice, a lower, warmer, mezzo than Abby's, carried farther across the midway. Abby cringed at the thought that this was her problem. Pitch was something she would have a hard time fixing. "You must hurry! Today and today only we have a sight of mystery and intrigue for you."

Passersby were turning and starting to gather. Abby had to try hard to temper the envy rising in her throat.

"Inside the tent," Ruth continued, dropping her voice to a conspiratorial stage whisper, "you will find displayed a discovery from the American desert, brought to us one night from other worlds unnamed. Step this way to the tent, please." She opened the flap and nodded Abby toward the opening so she could collect the ticket money as several townies hurried forward to pay.

Trying hard to keep her breath steady, Abby took their money and sent them in to where the fake aliens waited in their jars of noxious smelling liquid. When the last had passed through into the exhibit, she turned to Ruth. "How the hell did you do that?"

"I just wanted to make sure it wasn't the aliens." She peeked into the tent. The townies were all gasping appropriately. "And it's not you. It's just, I've watched plenty of these, after a while you start to see what people respond to."

"Did you ever do the bally? Or—what's your act, then?"

Ruth shook her head, picking up her box of lunches from where she set it down. She rummaged through and handed a small container of fried vegetables to Abby. "I just help out. Little bit of this. Little bit of that."

"Right," Abby said, taking the vegetables gratefully. The smell of them made her realize that she was hungry after all. After popping one of the breaded broccoli florets into her mouth, she looked out at the crowds milling about the midway. No one seemed to take any notice of her. She thought back to the day she had taken her siblings to the carnival, how she wouldn't let them anywhere near the *crazy people who were shouting at them*. If she could go back and live that day over, she would change a number of things, but first they would patronize every single vendor. She hated the feeling of being seen right through. She didn't want anyone else to feel that way. "Della says a carnival can't run with extra parts, but at the moment, I really feel like an extra part."

Ruth bit her lip. "Why don't you get up there and try again? Just pretend you're telling a story. It's much easier that way."

Abby didn't think it would be that easy for her, but she nodded and stepped up to the edge of the platform. She considered doing exactly as Ruth had done, but the thought of it sent her pulse racing. She couldn't imitate Ruth, and besides, people had already heard what Ruth had to say. She stared out at the crowd looking for people casually walking through, reading the painted banners that proclaimed "REAL!" in bold letters. Suddenly, an idea struck her. Perhaps she didn't know how to tell a story, but she could sing a story. She waited until the crowds had shifted enough to bring fresh ears past the bally platform and took a deep breath.

Then she sang, beginning with the aria that she had been working on so many weeks ago when she had run away. Faces turned curiously in her direction. With a nervous glance at Ruth she rushed on, substituting words about aliens, flying saucers, and New Mexico for Amina's joy at Elvino's return. Some of the syllables did not quite line up, and her voice faltered more than once on the higher notes, but she refused to allow herself to stop until she had completed the aria. When she had, not only did applause break out, but a significant portion of the crowd walked to the tent.

When they had bought their tickets and gone inside, Ruth watched Abby with a broad grin. "I don't know what to say. That was simply—"

Abby waved a hand for her to stop speaking. She was too busy trying to calm her heartbeat to pay attention.

"Is something the matter?" Ruth asked, putting her box down again and scrambling onto the platform.

Abby shook her head, knowing full well that if she looked as faint as she felt, there was no way that Ruth would believe her. She gasped down air for a few seconds before she heard Ruth speaking again.

"Stage fright."

"What?" Abby asked, turning to her.

"You have stage fright." This was not a question. Ruth had not allowed Abby any opportunity to deny it.

"I'm a waitress who sings opera," Abby said by means of protest.

"None of that means you don't have stage fright."

Not wanting to argue over something she knew was absolutely true, Abby took a seat on the edge of the platform, trying to keep herself steady. Ruth followed suit, smiling indulgently. "I'm impressed that you went for it at all, honestly. I would never have had the guts."

"That's not true," Abby scoffed. "You did great up there."

Ruth laughed. "I'm only here because I have stage fright. Never would have met Constance if I hadn't …" she trailed off; a look of bliss lit her face at the memory.

"You two seem very happy," Abby said, grateful for the opportunity to change the subject. It struck her as a somewhat odd thing to say. It was something people said to newlyweds, or golden anniversary couples, or new parents. Ruth and Constance were none of those things, and yet, Abby had the strangest sensation that they were all three at once.

Ruth glanced back at Abby and examined her face. Abby felt uncomfortable, unsure of what Ruth was looking for in her eyes, but then Ruth seemed to decide and nodded with a smile. "We are," she said. "I'm not going to say it's easy, even in a caravan of misfits like this one, but, yes, we're quite happy."

Abby wanted ask about the caravan of misfits, but the words that came out were quite different altogether. "I've never been in love," Abby said. Immediately, she regretted letting the words escape so easily.

"Never?" Ruth asked, raising a skeptical eyebrow.

"Well." Abby laughed. Once she would have been appalled to know she was capable of a laugh that sounded so hollow and bitter. "There was Frank, I suppose. He was handsome and gentlemanly. He sent flowers, all the time. I was certainly fond of him. More than fond, really. I thought I might marry him. Everyone did. But, it's hard to remember now, after everything that's happened."

Ruth nodded, listening, but not interjecting.

"He was always so … earnest? I don't know if that's the right word, but when he talked about how no one on earth would ever love me like he did, well, I honestly thought he meant it. He may have meant it. That doesn't make it true. Still, I believed him. So, when he left me for someone else …"

Ruth gently patted Abby on the arm.

"I fell apart, Ruth. I shattered. You would think that means that I loved him, but does it? Or did I just break like that because I believed him when he said he was the only one who'd have me?"

Instead of answering, Ruth pulled her friend into a silent hug.

"How did you know that you loved Constance? I mean, you're both girls—" a memory played at the back of her mind, a feeling of freedom, but she couldn't quite grab hold of it or recall where it came from, who it came from. "How could two girls know they love each other?"

"Same as any two people. It's different for everyone. I wish I could tell you how you know, but I could never distill into words how Constance makes me feel. It's just, when I look into the future and I think about my life, it's only right when she's there. Anything else feels … like telling a lie."

"When I look into my future, all I feel is a lot of nothing. What does that mean?"

"Like I said, it's different for everyone. Some people feel a faster heartbeat, some sweaty palms, others, maybe a rush of excitement, or I've heard from a very reliable source, the opposite, a sense of complete calm."

Abby had to smile. She couldn't help it. "What about a buzzing sensation right at the back of your skull?"

A smile softened Ruth's face. "I wouldn't rule it out. When was this?"

"It's nothing. I'm just … throwing out hypotheticals."

"Of course." Ruth nudged her shoulder playfully. "Well, I've got to get these lunches distributed before they get cold, and you've got some tickets to sell." She left Abby alone with her thoughts; it wasn't long before they drew an image of a statuesque woman with long, tousled, dark auburn hair.

THAT NIGHT ABBY ONCE AGAIN attempted, in vain, to stitch the seams of Della's costumes back together. The tight, glossy fabric that Abby couldn't name kept slipping from her hands. The thread constantly escaped the needle and, in the dim light of the trailer's single overhead fluorescent, Abby found it increasingly difficult to return it to its rightful place. When it happened yet again, she let out a cry of frustration, shoving the sea of fabric across the table and away from her.

She had been working at the fruitless task since Della left for her performance earlier in the evening. She didn't see how she was going to get anything accomplished, and she was sure that Della was catching on to that. So far, though, she hadn't said anything more than pointedly mentioning how much she'd like to be able to wear the purple outfit again in Chicago.

Outside, Abby heard a great cheer from somewhere in the camp. She lifted the blinds and looked around. Just over the top of the other nearby trailers, she could see the flames of a bonfire flicking their way toward the sky. Music started: a guitar, a saxophone, and perhaps a man's voice, though the words were too muffled for Abby to hear clearly, drifted through the lot. It sounded magical. Without a second thought, she abandoned her sewing and hurried off to investigate the source of the music.

The bonfire was impressive. Abby couldn't imagine where they had found so much fuel for it. She stood off to the side, watching as the rest of the carnival reveled before her. It was quite the sight, and it made her heart soar to see so many people so happy.

Distracted, she didn't feel the tiny tug at her hand until she heard Phebe's voice. "Come on, Aaabbyyy," she begged, trying her best to pull her in the direction of the bonfire.

Abby grinned down at the little girl. Now she sounded just like Annette. A wave of sadness brushed her at the thought of her baby sister, but she shook it off, following Phebe into the throng.

A mixture of hay bales and chairs formed a haphazard half-circle around the gigantic fire, though most seats had been abandoned as people danced nearby, where Constance's father crooned a lovely, mournful tune in a language Abby did not understand. She listened, transfixed, as Phebe happily swung her arm to the music.

Near the musicians, she noticed that Vinnie had just unpacked an accordion and was gesturing wildly to her. "Ah! *Si Maritau Rosa!*" he mouthed.

"He wants you to sing with him!" Phebe teased.

Abby sucked in a breath. She knew exactly what Vinnie wanted. He wanted her to laugh and run up there to sing a tarantella with him, but she didn't plan to do any such thing. She shook her head and mouthed, "No way!" back at him.

Phebe, however, had different plans. She tugged hard on Abby's arm, trying to drag her toward the musicians.

"No, Phebe," Abby begged, but Phebe did not listen. She pulled so hard that Abby had to walk with her or risk losing her arm.

Vinnie beamed when they reached the musicians.

"I don't really … remember many of the words," Abby confessed, feeling terribly sheepish. Her mother had sung this particular Sicilian folk song many times when she was little, but it had been quite some time since she had heard the tune.

"I'll start you off," he said, playing a few random notes and seeming unconcerned. "It'll come back to you."

Sure enough, the folk song did just that. More than that. *Vinni la primavera li mennuli sù n'ciuri. Lu focu di l'ammuri lu cori m'addurmò.* The words felt lively and lush, more at home in her voice than any opera song ever had. *E ammezzu suli e ciuri, avvolunu l'aceddi. Tutti 'sti cosi beddi mi fannu suspirà.* The melody rushed through her, lending strength with every note and erasing all of her nervousness. *Si maritau Rosa Saridda e Pippinedda e iù, ca sugnu bedda mi vogghiu marità.* When she finished, she gasped for air, flush with the high the song had given her. Vinnie was still beaming.

"Another?" he asked.

"Let me catch my breath."

He nodded, and she stumbled away from the musicians. She was on top of the world. Her body soared as if, from this moment forward, she could accomplish anything.

Her energy propelled her forward until she collapsed onto a hay bale. She breathed in her surroundings. It was a perfect night; everything around her seemed to glow in the firelight, and the night was as full of possibilities as stars. She gazed up at them. They seemed to have multiplied; there were never this many in Cleveland, and she had no idea how she had never noticed that. Still breathing deeply, trying to calm her body, she let her mind flit through Nonna Gaetana's stories: tales of dancing, and firelight, and the lovelorn mysteries that took place among the stars.

Seated not far away, she spotted Suprema nursing a soda bottle and watching the dancers' feet as they spun and twirled. She felt a strange stillness and smiled to herself. A surge of bravery holding her usual fears at bay, Abby stood up and before she realized that she had done it, she was walking toward her.

"Hi, Suprema?" she said, standing next to her with every nerve in her body firing fast and furious. The words came out sounding more like a question than an exclamation at seeing a friend. Mentally she kicked herself and was about to start again when Suprema looked away from the dancers.

She glanced up, a sardonic smile on her lips. "I don't even know why I bother coming out of my trailer when we do this."

Abby still wasn't sure how to respond, but she barreled on, "Not having fun?"

"Does it look like I'm having fun?"

"Well, I—"

"I mean look at them!" She gestured at the group of dancers. Abby recognized a few people, though she couldn't say their names. They all spun and swiveled, throwing in wild acrobatics as one might expect carnival performers to do. Most striking, though, were Ruth and Constance. They weren't dancing with any elaborate flourishes, but there was an elegant grace about the two of them. On one swung downbeat, Constance would nudge Ruth's arm onto her shoulder with her elbow and take her by the waist. The next, Ruth would do the same. The two of them glided like nymphs made of pure flame, turning and sliding their feet and their bodies without thought or hesitation. Abby was mystified. She had never learned to lead, not with an older brother and a boyfriend like Frank, and the very thought of needing to be decisive with dance steps boggled her mind. Still, knowledge of steps didn't seem to play the slightest role in the way Ruth and Constance danced, which seemed like a supernaturally seamless communication, as if they were reading each other's minds.

"How do they do that?"

Suprema shrugged. "Wish I knew. Girls like me don't get asked to dance."

Abby wanted to say, "I'm sure that's not true," but she managed to stop herself. Suprema, of all people, would know much better than Abby whether or not people asked her to dance. Still, she didn't want her to feel that way, not tonight, not when she herself felt like rising into the sky. She stood for a while, watching the other couples. Then an idea struck her. Just as she had seen done by Fred Astaire in any number of movies, she held out her hand, palm up, with a flourish. "Could I have the honor of this dance?"

Suprema stared blankly, her eyes narrowed, her shoulders turned in what almost seemed like fear. Abby held her ground, not moving her proffered hand from its position even when it started to shake. Her heart pounded in her ears, but she couldn't take back her hand now, not when she wasn't fully sure that she could move.

Ever so slowly, the mixture of bewilderment and trepidation began to dissolve. "Is this some kind of joke?" Suprema asked, her voice still unsure.

"Not even slightly."

"I'm a really bad dancer."

"Why would that matter to me? Does it matter to you?"

A small smile tugged at the corners of Suprema's mouth, but it didn't fully form. Instead, she nodded and stood, taking Abby's hand. "I'm honestly not very good," she said in a resigned monotone. "Just warning you."

"Neither am I," Abby answered. An electrical charge of excitement zipped through her as they walked to where the others were dancing. "I have no idea how to lead, but Natale always complained that I led him, so … maybe I can figure something out."

"No one ever bothered to teach me. Not even to follow." Suprema blushed and looked at her feet.

Abby shook her head. "My nonna says the key to dancing is just to feel the music and let go of everything else. You can worry about getting the steps right later. The more you think, the worse you'll be." She hoped that Nonna Gaetana was right.

Vinnie started again on the accordion. Instead of a tarantella, he played "Why Do Fools Fall in Love?" at a much more languid tempo than Abby had ever heard it. The juxtaposition of styles made both girls laugh. "See, who could not dance to this?" Abby teased.

Suprema answered with a smile, and the pair began to twirl through the crowd. Though both had been worried that their lack of skill would draw mockery, no one pointed, no one laughed. Abby was enthralled, watching the smile on her dancing partner's face. And for the first time, Abby was at one with the carnival, as though she finally belonged there. In that instant everything from the heat of the bonfire to Suprema's hands in hers was perfect and right. It wouldn't last. In fact, she was almost positive that come morning, she would feel as lost and desperate to get home as ever, but for this one night, she was willing to let go and feel the music.

~December, 1946~

Now that he's come home from the war, Abby waits up every night for her Papa to come home from work. He had been gone so long that now, even though she knows where he is, she needs to see him before she can sleep. She needs him to ruffle her hair and say, "Topolina, are you still awake?" in his incredulous voice, as if he's not expecting it. She needs this, or her dreams will be icy, and cold, and dark.

Mama waits up too. She washes the dishes and sweeps the floor in silence, as if she is afraid to make a sound. She used to sing. Abby notices but does not understand. Mama does not notice Abby as she sits on the stairs and listens to the same silence.

That night, Abby must have fallen asleep, because she does not hear Papa come home. Instead, she hears hushed voices in the kitchen. Mama and Papa are talking, but Abby cannot hear them. She sneaks farther down by inches, squinting as if that will keep the stairs from creaking. She has done this before, but that was different. That was before. Now, Papa is home and can protect them.

"You're so quiet now, *cara mia*. What has the war done to you?" Abby hears Papa ask. She peers into the kitchen to see him seated at the table, holding Mama's hands. His eyes are sad and tired.

Mama shakes her head. She whispers, and Abby has to strain her ears to hear her. She cranes her neck, though she doesn't think it will help. "Nothing's been the same since they made you go away," are the only words Abby can make out.

"Yes." Papa lets go of her hands and rests them on the table. "You don't sing and I worry … is it my fault?"

Mama's eyes flash, in the bright angry way they do when Abby and Natale come home covered in mud or bother the baby. Then the flash changes to the cold, frightened, rapid blinking that happens when people she doesn't know approach them on the street. "It is hard to sing when you feel so alone." Her words are louder, but slower, more stilted, spoken with more care to hide their usual melody.

Papa stands and walks around the table to where she is seated. She wraps her arms around her chest as if to protect herself. Hidden on the stairs, Abby is almost afraid to breathe. "Even when you're here, you're not here," her mama continues. "You're a different man."

"Do you want me to go?" Papa asks. His voice is so sad, sadder than Abby can remember it being.

He brightens a little when Mama shakes her head. Then she says something Abby doesn't quite understand.

"I'm expecting again." Her words fight with each other, as if she is unsure how to feel.

Papa hesitates. Abby thinks that he is about to throw his arms wide and lift Mama into the air. Maybe even spin her with joy. She remembers when they used to do this before he went away. He doesn't, though. He stops halfway, watching her face to decide his next move.

Tears begin to trail down Mama's face, and it is all Abby can do to stay where she is hidden. "I want to be able to sing for my children, but I can't do it anymore."

Abby wants to hug her. She needs to hold on to her mother and tell her everything is going to be okay, just as her mother does for her every time she has a nightmare, and she had so many nightmares when Papa was away. She starts to stand, eager to race to her.

"Cara—"

"I want to promise them a world full of beauty and music. How can I promise them that?" She sounds frantic and that makes Abby's heart pound.

"Mama?" she whispers, but they do not hear her. She isn't surprised. She can barely hear herself. She takes a few creaky steps into the kitchen. Papa could see her now if he were to look away from Mama's eyes. "Mama?" she says again.

Abby's does not know whether or not her parents see her standing there. Papa says, "Promises are something for weak men to hide behind. The only thing we can do is live."

Those words ring through Abby's mind all night and will echo for years to come.

Chapter Twelve

Torrential rain and muddy fields greeted the caravan in Indiana. Setup had stalled almost immediately with no solid foothold for the rides, booths, or tents. After stepping out and sinking ankle-deep in a murky puddle, Della refused to leave the trailer until the whole of South Bend had dried out—even when Vivian arrived with an extra coat and umbrella.

"What's the point?" Della asked of the poor girl standing on her trailer steps, huddled as close as she could to the door, trying to stay out of the rain. "There's nothing in this town except self-important university boys."

"You can't stay in this trailer the whole week."

"If it rains all week, we'll move on."

Abby listened, waiting for the right moment to jump in and take the offered umbrella for herself. She wanted to walk somewhere, anywhere, that wasn't Della's cramped and cluttered trailer. The entire day, she had been pretending to sew clumps of tulle onto a skirt. If Della had taken it, she would have seen nothing but a rather fluffy ball of fabric and haphazard stitches, but Abby wasn't about to let that happen, at least not until she was able to track down Thomas. Even if they weren't putting on a show, they would have received some mail.

"At least come play cards with me and the girls. No one else around here knows euchre."

"I'm not going anywhere. You girls can come here if you're bored."

Vivian rolled her eyes and tried to force her way past Della into the trailer.

"Watch it! You're gonna get water on everything!"

"Then keep the place cleaner!" Vivian cried, sticking the umbrella into the trailer as Della tried to shut the door on her.

"None of your business!" Della pushed hard and cracked a few of the umbrella's wire arms.

"This is not accomplishing anything," Abby muttered, but Della did not acknowledge her.

"Stop being so stubborn!"

Abby's hand slipped, and she jabbed her finger with the sewing needle. She bit back a yelp, but Della and Vivian seemed to have heard it. They ceased their struggle at the door and turned to her. Embarrassed, she shoved the fluffy mess of tulle under her pillow and stood up. "I'm done with this. If you need a fourth, Vivian, I'll play."

Vivian glanced at Della with a somewhat satisfied smirk. "You play euchre?"

"I'm not good," Abby said with a shrug. "But I can't focus on sewing cooped up in here."

"You can't focus on sewing ever," Della said, a hint of bitterness creeping into her voice. "I have half a mind to—" but she didn't have time to finish her sentence. Abby had slipped past her without so much as a word, taken Vivian's somewhat battered umbrella, and ducked out the door into the rain. Della wasn't about to follow them.

The bent arms of the umbrella caused water to cascade over Abby's left shoulder. She tipped it even more, hoping not to get any wetter than necessary or to direct the flow of rainwater toward Vivian.

"I don't really play, you know," Abby confessed after they had been walking in dreary silence for a minute. "I just needed to get out of there."

Vivian shrugged. "I figured." They continued in silence, until she burst out, "I don't know what the hell has gotten into her!"

Abby stopped walking and stared at Vivian, who was clutching her umbrella so tight it seemed she might snap the metal base in half.

She continued. "At first I thought she was into you or something, and finding out you were hooking up with Wonder Woman put her off."

Abby's face turned several different shades of red as she tried to stammer out, "We were only dancing," but her vocal cords would not obey. Just thinking about Vivian's words made Abby feel as if she had been drinking too much champagne.

Vivian raised an eyebrow, and Abby scrambled to cover her expression. "Oh, come on, don't look like that. This is a carnival, not a church social. And you're making me sound like Trixie."

"Della's… no different than usual." Abby managed to force out. The words weren't close to what she wanted to say, what she wanted to know.

"Like hell she isn't." Vivian began to pace through the mud. Her bright yellow rain boots were slicked with it up to her ankles. "Look, you don't know her like I do. That girl's been my best friend since day one, and this is not her. She doesn't refuse to come out in the rain. She runs through the rain and laughs at you if you won't go with her."

Abby didn't know what to say. It was true she didn't know Della all that well, despite spending a significant amount of time around her, but the problem still didn't seem as serious to her as Vivian seemed to believe it was.

"Did your brother break up with her?" Vivian asked, pausing in her pacing.

"I don't—" Abby stopped as well, thinking, but if she hadn't heard from Natale, she doubted that Della had either. Della would have taunted her about it, she was sure of it. "But I don't see why—"

"No," Vivian interrupted. "She would have told me. Maybe it's her parents. God, I wish that girl would talk."

"I thought her parents—I thought she had a lot of boyfriends. Why would Natale matter?"

Vivian didn't answer. She looked at Abby as if she had a lot to say, but she didn't answer.

The rain continued to pound down around them, and the wind was beginning to pick up. The days had been warm, but not nearly warm enough to let people stand around in the rain as long as they had. Vivian was shaking with cold. Abby looked around at the entire grounds, still wrapped up like a discarded present.

"Maybe she just wants to start working again," she suggested.

"Don't we all?" Vivian frowned, her eyes making the same circuit over the dismal, damp carnival lot that Abby's just had. "Look, you can go back if you want. No need to drag yourself down there. The food tent keeps slipping in the mud, plus it's drafty."

"You said you needed a fourth."

"No offense, but if I needed a partner, I wouldn't pick Della. Plenty of people play. Vinnie's good; that's how we met him. And heck, even Pasternak, who insists she only plays Jass, is actually a better hand at the game than Della."

"Then why—?"

"Why do you think?"

Abby still didn't want to go back. She didn't want to have to deal with Della at the moment, good mood or bad. "Who all will be there then?"

"Anyone in particular you're wondering about?" Vivian's eyes twinkled, and Abby felt herself begin to blush again.

"No."

"Well, then I guess you're going to have to come and see. I don't keep a guest list." Abby had to look away so she wouldn't see the playful grin dancing across Vivian's face.

When the girls finally got to the food tent, Abby wished she had taken Vivian up on the offer to turn back. The tent provided some shelter from the rain, except where it leaked through a hole around the center pole and dripped steadily into a large puddle. The few tables that had been set up were moved to the side, away from the ever-growing pool, but it was slowly encroaching on a few of them. At the farthest table, a huddled group had gathered. Abby didn't recognize many of them, so she assumed they must be in charge of rides or concessions. Of course, it was easy enough to guess that the towering gentleman was "Marty the human giant," to whom Celia had once referred.

"Deal us in, boys!" Vivian called out to the group, which was actually mixed in gender.

"You'll have to wait 'til this round's over, love," a ride jockey called back.

"Won't be long. Marty and me are in the barn," added a woman's voice, a voice that Abby knew well, Suprema's voice. Abby's heart jumped.

Vivian and Abby moved closer, and Abby began to differentiate people from the mass: the older gentleman who had played guitar for Constance's father sat next to Suprema, and a concessions vendor whom Ruth had introduced to her was opposite her. Abby had forgotten her name, but she made delicious calzones.

"My money's on sideshow," Vivian laughed, and a few people groaned.

"Too late to bet," said Vinnie, who had been leaning against one of the nearby tent poles, watching the action. He caught Abby's eye and winked, shaking a still smoldering but mostly damp cigar as if to scold them for arriving late.

Abby turned away, allowing her gaze to shift to Suprema. She tried to catch her eye or send a smile of encouragement her way, but she seemed intent upon on her cards. After much consideration, she put a ten of hearts on the center of the table. The spectators raised eyebrows, but when the next cards were played—a king of diamonds, a queen of clubs, and a nine of hearts—and Suprema scooped them up with relish, they began to understand what was happening.

"You've got 'em all, don't you?" Marty hissed.

"No table talk!" shouted the guitar player, looking defeated.

"But you know she does."

"I do." Suprema laid out the rest of her hand, a whole set of hearts: jack, king, queen, and ace. "Read 'em and weep, gents."

The other two groaned, but Marty held his hand out for Suprema to shake. She did so, beaming. That was when Abby finally caught her eye. Immediately, Suprema's cheeks reddened, and she dropped her eyes to the table.

'Well, I'm out," she said, standing up and grabbing the umbrella that had been propped against the bench. Not listening to a single protest, she hurried off into the rain. Vinnie stamped his cigar the rest of the way out and raced after her at breakneck speed.

"Lovers' spat?" Vivian asked in a low whisper, but Abby couldn't answer. She felt cold inside.

Abby stayed at the food tent, waiting for the rain to diminish so she could go back and face Della. Even after it trailed off to a light mist, she remained. All she could bring herself to do was lean against the pole where Vinnie had been and, without paying much attention, watch the euchre players fade in and out of the game. Her thoughts were preoccupied with Suprema's cold brush-off. She supposed it didn't seem out of character for her, and yet, after the dance in Kalamazoo, Abby had been hoping for a much different reception the next time she saw her, though part of her couldn't say why. She didn't know what she expected from Suprema or even what she wanted. All she knew was the way she felt around her, as if her skin had come alive and everything she ever wanted was just around the corner; as if life were a Buddy Holly song.

"Psst! Abby!" Vinnie called out, breaking through her fog of thoughts. She shook her head. "You in there, Abby?"

Abby frowned and looked back at him. He was carrying an umbrella, but he hadn't unfurled it. He looked ridiculous standing there, soaked to the bone and yet still holding an umbrella. She bit back a laugh, unsure if his appearance was meant to be as funny as it struck her.

"Come on, at least giggle at the shoes," he said, holding the umbrella out for Abby.

She hadn't noticed his shoes. They were far too covered in mud to be distinguished from the ground. "I'm sure I will when I can see them. What's going on?"

"I was wondering if you were in the mood for some pizza?"

Vivian put her cards down and turned toward them. There was a flash of protectiveness in her eyes that Abby hadn't seen since her last night at the diner. "Abby's playing cards with me, Vinnie," she said, that note of vigilance flowing through her voice as well. Though Abby knew that Vinnie was her friend, she had to admit she appreciated it, especially from Vivian, whom she did not know well. She wondered if the burlesque girls were used to having to act as each other's protectors.

"Thanks, Vivian," Abby said, trying to let her know that her words were appreciated. "But I really could go for some decent pizza right now. I'm starving."

Vivian looked Abby over with raised, skeptical eyebrows, then shrugged and went back to her card game.

"So, pizza then?" Abby asked, taking Vinnie's umbrella.

Vinnie's laugh sounded nervous, but Abby chose to ignore that. "Well, I never said it was going to be decent, but it will be pizza."

Chapter Thirteen

When Abby and Vinnie arrived at the tiny, hidden-away pizza parlor, he grew very quiet. "H-here we are," he said, opening the door for her.

Abby stared at him before stepping inside. His hands were shaking. That seemed unlike him. Still, she didn't know him well. Perhaps this pizza parlor was the site of some long-ago trauma, or perhaps he saw someone inside that he knew. "Is something wrong?"

He shook his head and gestured awkwardly into the restaurant with his still-quavering arm. "Go on in."

"Why do I get the feeling that you're reluctantly sending me before a firing squad?"

Frowning, Vinnie went ahead into the restaurant. He walked toward a booth near the back. There sat Suprema, sipping soda from a glass. She looked up at them with a smile. The smile jarred Abby. She stepped forward casually, but before she could say hello, Vinnie jumped in and said, "Well, here we are; you two kids enjoy," and rushed out the door.

Abby stared after him, then took a seat in the booth opposite Suprema. She smiled at her because she truly was happy to see her, but Vinnie's actions were confusing. Why ask her for pizza and then run away? Why not tell her that Suprema would be there? It seemed like an ambush. "He's not coming back, is he?" she asked.

"I don't think so," Suprema said and glanced at the door. "He … probably thinks you're gonna hate him, or worse, never sing with him again."

This puzzled Abby all the more, who looked around the pizza parlor with increasing confusion. It was a simple restaurant with booths along the wall, a few scattered tables, and a glass display counter. The decorations were sparse, just a few Italian flags and red, green, and white checked tablecloths. The counter exhibited a number of pastries that looked quite appetizing: delicately beautiful pistachio-encrusted cannoli, fig *cucciddati* iced in shades of pink and green, and, in the center of the case, a deeply impressive *cassatta* decorated with intricate marzipan figurines. Abby's mouth watered.

She looked at Suprema. "I give. Why would he think bringing me here would make me hate him?"

Suprema fidgeted with her napkin ring and did not meet Abby's eyes.

Abby didn't want to push, so she stayed quiet, looking over the menu, which was full of dishes which made her homesick, but far from angry with anyone, especially Vinnie.

"I asked him to bring you," Suprema blurted.

Abby lowered her menu. "What do you mean?"

With her pale face and wide eyes, Suprema looked even more nervous than Abby felt on stage. "I was afraid," she said, speaking slowly and deliberately, "that if I asked you, you wouldn't want to come."

Abby pondered what to say. It was true that she didn't know what to make of Suprema and the way that she made her feel. The more time she spent with her, the more she liked being around her, the more she felt the funny buzz in the back of her skull and the leaping fish in her stomach. "I don't know. I might have said yes. You did dance with me, after all."

Suprema's cheeks reddened further. "I know. That's why I thought you'd say no."

"I enjoyed our dance," Abby confessed. A worm of doubt began to squirm in her gut, nagging at the fish, making them leap all the more. Abby had had a lovely time, but perhaps she had been even worse at leading than she thought. Was that why Suprema had been so cold at the card game?

"I'm not exactly graceful," Suprema said.

"Neither am I."

"That's not true. You move right. Me? I'm too tall and I step wrong and I'm like a bull in a china shop. It's awful."

Abby frowned and watched Suprema's face. It was almost a mask, as if Suprema didn't want her to read the true emotions hidden there. "I really did enjoy dancing with you," Abby said in a voice that sounded more forced than she would have liked.

"So did I!" Suprema said. Her voice had shifted from self-deprecation to a sincere urgency. "I didn't mean to imply that I didn't. I did. I really did. That's why I—well, it's silly now."

"I like silly things too," Abby tried to tease, then winced at her own lack of wit.

"I've never been on a date before, but I can tell this isn't going all that well."

It hit Abby like an icicle to the eye. She stared, stunned, at the lovely woman seated across from her. This was supposed to be a date. She couldn't parse it. She had felt an attraction to Suprema. She knew that. She had known ever since she had discussed her love life with Ruth, but to hear it laid out in such plain, clear terms... She was on a date. She and Frank had gone on dates. They had gone to movie theaters and dances and pizza parlors just like this one.

Still, clarity eluded her. She blinked, trying to block her racing thoughts and settle on the moment. Right now. This second. Suprema had asked her here. This was a date. She was happy. She was intrigued. The buzzing sounded less like bees and more like the purr of a cat. "I didn't know," she whispered.

"Vinnie didn't—?"

"Vinnie didn't explain anything. He just asked me if I was in the mood for pizza."

Suprema sighed. "I'm sorry, I just—I like you, and I thought, maybe, you'd like me too. I should have known—"

Abby reached across the table and took her hand. "You have got to stop doing that." Moving purely on instinct, she looked Suprema in the eyes. She found the irises, where shades of blue faded into gray, mesmerizing. "How about we just order a pizza and see how this goes?"

Suprema looked back at her for a long while. Then she let out a long breath and smiled. "Yes, I think I would like that."

Abby ordered a mushroom pizza with just a few anchovies because Suprema made a face when she mentioned them. Just as Vinnie had implied, the pizza turned out to be a mouth-burningly hot, thick-crusted, far-too-cheesy monstrosity, but Abby did not mind. In fact, as she took her first bite, she closed her eyes and smiled. Her Nonna's pizza was nothing like this, but that didn't matter. That was a pizza from her home and her family. This was a pizza that she was sharing with Suprema.

"You're much easier to please than Vinnie," Suprema said with a light laugh. "I don't think we've ever had a pizza without him whining about it."

Abby had to laugh. Vinnie seemed exactly like the kind of person who would do that. She took another bite of the pizza and watched Suprema's face. She seemed so shy, so unlike the girl who had stormed through the carnival tent on that first day. "Suprema, if it helps, you can pretend that—"

"Would you like me to put a song on the jukebox?" she asked, quickly.

Abby's eyes lit up. She missed having a jukebox around. "Yes, please."

"Which song?"

"Play your favorite."

Suprema went over to the jukebox and flipped through the titles. She seemed to carefully examine and consider each one, which brought a smile to Abby's face. Her days as a waitress at the Cedar Road Diner had taught her a lot about how to read people from the way they chose a song at the jukebox. There were the spontaneous types, who selected the first interesting record they came to; the extra-spontaneous types who just punched in a random number; the indecisive types who stood, barely reading the titles, until a crowd formed and began to complain; the type that asked everyone for suggestions; the decisive type that knew exactly what they wanted to hear; and Suprema's type, the analytic type that chose carefully in order to convey exactly the right message. Such people made pro-con lists and took decisions seriously. They didn't ask girls out on dates unless they were sure they felt something for them. A blush rose on Abby's cheeks. Then the first strains of "Why Do Fools Fall in Love?" floated through the restaurant, and Abby's blush deepened.

"This is your favorite song?" she asked in a squeaky voice when Suprema returned.

Suprema nodded, also blushing. "It is now."

Abby's shyness made her afraid to say anything. She fought it, bit her lip, and then barreled forward. "I didn't realize how much I missed music," she said. Suprema glanced around the restaurant, then touched her hand as if to say "go on." "Before the carnival, my life was all music. Opera during the day. My mother's folk songs or the diner jukebox at night. Now? Della doesn't even have a radio. I don't think I've heard a new song since I left Cleveland, and I used to listen to Moondog nightly."

"And here I thought you were all sophistication, Abby Amaro," Suprema teased.

Abby smiled. Her confidence was coming back. "Hardly. I wore bobby socks and saddle shoes like any other girl. I just, I was pretty focused on trying to make something of myself."

"As an opera singer?"

"Yeah. Sounds kinda silly now, doesn't it?"

"Not at all." Suprema took another bite of her pizza, but Abby could feel her eyes on her. That made her stomach squirm, but in a good, butterfly-filled way. She hadn't felt that queasy rush since she and Marjorie had joked about running away to New York. "I have a radio. You could come listen any time."

"I'd like that." Frankie Lymon's voice faded, and Abby jumped to her feet. "My turn?"

"Do you have a favorite song?"

"That would be like asking me to choose a favorite child, but I do have the last song I fell in love with." She squeezed Suprema's hand before taking her own coins over to the brightly colored record player. She usually wasn't the decisive type. She was more of a "let other people choose the songs and stay far away from the machine" type. This time, however, she had a very specific song in mind. She selected it immediately and watched as the mechanical arm plucked the little red-orange 45 with "Coral" printed in bold letters from the pack. It had been May when she first heard the song. May had been a hard month: breaking up with Frank, being made an understudy for yet another season. But then she had heard this song on the radio and it made her think that maybe, just maybe, something good was coming down the line. She popped in her dime and pressed the button. The sounds of a guitar, a celeste, and Buddy Holly's voice filled the pizza parlor.

She glanced back at Suprema with a bright, bold smile. Suprema returned the expression.

Abby scurried back to finish her pizza.

They ate the rest of their dinner in silence, each occasionally glancing up to look at the other and blushing just a little. Everything felt sweet and new, and Abby reveled in it, though a nagging voice told her that she probably shouldn't. She knew well enough how sweet and new could turn out. She shook off the anxious, warning voice by focusing on the purr-like buzz and the fact that Suprema had chosen to play their first dance song.

"We should probably get back," Suprema said abruptly after the silence had dragged on for quite some time. "Heaven only knows when the show will pack up, but it's bound to be soon."

Abby stood up from the table and offered her arm to Suprema, who took it with a raised eyebrow. "Do you think they will? We're supposed to be here another three days according to the route card."

"Oh, those things aren't gospel," Suprema said as they made their way out into the rain. Abby lifted the umbrella and it covered them both easily, despite their height discrepancy. "We pack up early for plenty of reasons. Overbearing laws, slow crowds." She stuck her hand out from under the umbrella and waved her fingers in the rain. "And especially bad weather. Nothing worse than bad weather."

"How long have you been with the carnival?" Abby ventured, not sure whether or not the question was considered too personal. Constance had said that carnival folk didn't like to talk about themselves, after all.

Suprema gave Abby an appraising look, her eyes searching much in the way Ruth's had. "Since I was thirteen," she said. Her words were slow, as if she were dropping a weight with each one. "Uncle Boleslaw and his wife brought me. I like to think I took to it pretty quickly."

"Did something happen to your parents?"

This question she didn't answer. Instead, she slipped her hand into Abby's and squeezed it, holding on tight as they walked back in a contented silence. Abby didn't know what to think. Her head was swimming, and each of the raindrops hitting the sidewalk in the intensifying storm matched a confused thought. And yet her hand was tucked safely in Suprema's; somehow, that felt more right than anything.

~September, 1956~

The diner is thinning out for the night. There are only a few stragglers in their booths, and Abby is already sweeping the floor behind the counter, preparing to close.

"So, are you going to the dance at the lakeshore next weekend?" Marjorie asks, leaning over the counter.

Abby shakes her head. "It's so embarrassing to go by yourself."

"That's the point. You're supposed to meet people there," Marjorie says with a laugh. She ruffles a hand through her red curls, pulling them out of her waitress ponytail, and Abby wonders if she'll ask if they can go together. With someone as pretty as Marjorie around, people would be more likely to approach them.

"I don't know. They say that, but every time I've gone, everyone else was there as a couple, and people stare at you if you stand at the wall too long."

Marjorie purses her lips, then nods toward one of the booths of stragglers. It is a group of boys in a mixture of blazers and leather jackets, as if they couldn't decide if they were a gang or a fraternity. "Maybe you should ask one of them. They're cute."

"Marjorie!" Abby exclaims, louder than she means to. Some of the boys turn to look. She lowers her voice to a hiss. "Marjorie. I can't just—"

"Why not? If we've always gotta wait around for them, we're not gonna get anywhere."

Abby stops sweeping and looks at the booth again, trying to keep her eyes down so that she does not appear obvious. The one with soft hazel eyes is looking right at her, and his smile is disarming. She turns around as fast as she can.

"He's coming over here," Marjorie whispers seconds before giggling and rushing away.

"Marjorie!" Abby hisses after her, but it is too late. She is gone.

"Excuse me?" The boy with hazel eyes asks. Abby takes a deep breath and turns to face him. "I'm Frank. Frank Butler."

Abby nods. "I know who you are," she says, and then, embarrassed, closes her eyes

Frank just laughs. "I do come in here too much, don't I?"

"No, I—"

"I couldn't help overhearing," he says before she can continue. "I will take you to the neighborhood dance."

Abby looks him over. The fact that he says "I will" instead of "may I" registers, but she tries to push it away. She feels light inside. "All right."

Chapter Fourteen

Za Teresa,

I know that the fault for not writing sooner lies with me and that things between all of us have been strained of late. I hope you can forgive me. I have been thinking a great deal about happier memories and as I will be traveling through Chicago in the coming week, I would like very much to see you. You can reach me at Post Office Box #MC-36011 Chicago, 2, if you wish to let me know when you might be available for me to call on you. I would so like to try some of your marzipan once again.

Tutti amuri,
Abby Amaro
Ninfa's oldest girl

Suprema had been correct. The caravan was given the word to leave South Bend the very next day. While the news made Abby anxious, Della seemed quite excited by the change of pace.

"I don't see the point," Abby complained as the trailer and the rest of the caravan barreled up US-20. She had hoped to catch a glimpse or two of Lake Michigan or the often-discussed Indiana Dunes, but all she could see out the window was a thick, dreary rain. "Any weather that's causing problems in Indiana is probably causing the same problems in Chicago."

Della did not look at her. She was far too focused on the unpleasant road before her, but she did scoff. "Chicago's different. Chicago's big time."

"But it's still going to be raining there."

"Oh, you can predict the weather now, can you, Amaro?"

"I'm just saying—"

"Maybe you should stop just saying and shut up so I can concentrate."

Abby turned away and continued trying in vain to get a glimpse of the lakeshore. Rain-slicked roads aside, she was beginning to see that Vivian was right. Della had never been her best friend; Abby had known that on day one, but Della had tried to be nice in her own way. Now, she did seem to be growing increasingly irritable. More than anything, Abby wanted to ask what was bothering her, to see if, maybe, it had something to do with the lack of word from Natale, which was bothering her as well, but she didn't want to risk upsetting her any further.

She let her mind drift, thinking of her last trip to Chicago, of how Suprema's hand had felt so nice in hers, of marzipan, and of whether or not Suprema would like marzipan.

"Can you stop humming?" Della asked.

Abby turned to her and frowned. It was going to be a long drive.

CHICAGO SEEMED QUITE DIFFERENT FROM Abby's memories. That Chicago had been a misty haven of almond flavoring and her mother's espresso-tinged kisses. It had been an escape, a place where she and her family could hide away from the real world for just a little while. This Chicago smelled.

Della had been right. Chicago was different from their previous locations. The area where they set up the carnival was solid and well-kept. Despite having clearly received at least some of the same rain that had plagued them in Indiana, the ground was not too soft and muddy to set up. The problem, however, was in the air.

The field in which the caravan made camp was just downwind of something Abby could only describe as a garbage dump. Most of the time, it was unobtrusive. No one could see the source of the smell and, surrounded by the usual carnival delights of French fries, funnel cake, and popcorn, few seemed to notice. Still, every once in a while the wind would change direction and blow the usual smells away, replacing them with scents like dead fish heads and abandoned TV dinners and something far too ammonia-like.

The advance man had been roundly reprimanded. Rumors spread that he had been fired or even beaten. He rarely showed his face after the first whiffs came in, so it was hard to confirm or deny them. Chicago was supposed to be a big-money town, the biggest on their route card. They had even picked up a brand new big-ticket attraction: a real roller coaster. The smell never lasted long enough to fully drive away the crowds, and Chicago had enough people to make up for any locals who knew what the area smelled like. Still, the performers and vendors were not quiet in their complaints.

Abby sat perched on her bally platform, staring out at the midway, waiting for just the right moment to begin her song. She had been getting bolder, incorporating popular tunes and folk songs into her opera repertoire, and people seemed to be responding to it. Earlier today, she had managed to get a crowd of fifteen into the tent. At the edge of the row, she spotted her marks: a gaggle of teenagers walking away from the spinning strawberries ride and looking a little woozy. She struck her note and watched for a sign that she had their attention—a turned head, a raised eyebrow, an elbow to the ribs-—before beginning her brand-new interpretation of "Blue Suede Shoes." She referred to it as "Flying Saucer Blues."

The teenagers laughed and started over. Abby grinned in triumph until she saw the tomato. For a split second, it seemed as though all time had stopped. The tomato was bright scarlet red, too red, and Abby knew it was overripe. It hit her square in the stomach and burst open. The red juices looked like blood as they spattered across the yellow dress Ruth had found for her. The teenagers were laughing. A yelp of pain and humiliation had escaped Abby before she could stop it.

"Oh, my land!" one of the teenagers cried. "That's a real person!"

Abby wanted to shout back that of course she was, but she couldn't find the muscles to make her mouth move.

"Of course she's a real person!" roared a voice that did not belong to Abby. Coming from the back of the tent was Suprema, already dressed in her sideshow costume, which consisted of a leopard-print leotard and bone-shaped jewelry made of plastic. The group turned and ran in a cartoonish flash. "Are you all right?" Suprema asked, turning to Abby.

A few seconds passed. Abby found it hard to say a word. She touched the red stain and scraped at it with her hand, bringing up a glob of seeds. She inhaled and held the breath a few moments before speaking. "I'm fine, but I don't think the dress will make it through."

Suprema smiled as she helped her climb down from the platform. "Those kids were stupid."

Abby didn't know what to say. She touched the tomato stain again and sighed. "I'm sorry you had to rescue me. I—"

"Don't mention it." Suprema shook her head and began to unfurl the "Attraction Closed" sign and the rope that Abby was supposed to string across the tent entrance at the end of the day. "I came to see if you would beg off for a little while and come see my act."

There was something shy about her tone, but Abby was happy that she had come to find her instead of sending Vinnie or waiting for chance to bring them together again. "I would love to," Abby answered.

"It starts in a minute or two, but I'm the third act, so there's time, if you want to go change or—"

Abby squeezed her hand. "Lead the way. I'll make you look extra scary."

Suprema blushed and, for a split second, Abby thought she was about to giggle.

When Abby slipped into the dimly lit, forest-like atmosphere of the sideshow tent, she was disoriented. It took her a little too long to recognize Ruth waving her over. Abby hurried toward her, hoping to get away from probing eyes.

"What happened to you?" Ruth asked, her tone hushed and her eyes wide. She was clearly concerned, and Abby was very aware of how the red stain must look in the tent's misleading light.

Abby blushed. "I'll do everything I can to clean it or buy you a new one if I have to."

"No, I mean," Ruth looked around as if checking for eavesdroppers. "Do you need a doctor? We can probably get someone decent to come down for once if—"

"No! It's tomato!"

Someone in front of them turned and made a shushing motion, then saw Abby's dress and quickly turned back to face front.

Ruth burst into a fit of laughter and patted Abby on the back of the hand. "Your first tomato. Oh, Constance will be so proud of you. I haven't been tomatoed yet."

"Are you serious?"

Ruth just smiled back at her as the curtain opened and out walked the first act of the ten-in-one: Seven-foot-tall Marty, with his jeans deliberately hemmed too short to make him look even taller.

"Ruth?" Abby hissed, trying not to disrupt those around her, though they had been packed in.

"Hmm?"

"How come Marty didn't get in trouble in Michigan?"

Ruth shrugged. "When it comes to that so-called anti-monstrosity law, everything's too subjective to even guess."

A silence passed between them as they watched Marty walk around and pick up items that had been designed to look miniature in his hands. Ruth had obviously seen the act a few times, as she kept a muttered tally of tiny changes that he had chosen to make. "Ah, yes, breaking the teacup didn't get much of a laugh last time, true."

Abby didn't understand what the crowd of people found humorous about a man who was in obvious distress about not fitting into his world, but maybe the character Marty was playing was just hitting too close to home for her own comfort.

"Ruth?" she whispered again.

"Yeah?"

"Do you ever feel like you don't fit here?"

Ruth turned from her analysis of Marty's humor and looked at Abby. Her eyes were soft and warm, just as they had been when they had first met. "I don't really think about it all that much, I guess, but I suppose everyone feels that way sometimes."

"I was just thinking about how you don't really have an act, so you're just here because of, well..." she trailed off, unsure of how to voice her thoughts without possibly offending Ruth. Marty hustled off the stage. He was replaced by Boleslaw, who strategically poked pins into his face; the crowd gasped with each one.

"Constance," Ruth filled in after Abby had remained silent through four pin placements. "I'm here because of Constance. That is correct."

"I didn't mean to imply—"

"I'm not offended, Abby. It's true. I love Constance. Still, though, I wouldn't be here if I didn't want to be, if it wasn't the right place for me."

The entire audience let out a horrified cry as Boleslaw placed a pin dangerously close to his eye.

"Man's gonna blind himself one of these days," Ruth muttered.

Abby wanted to say more. She wanted to ask Ruth if it was okay to stay—even if she didn't feel quite at home in a place where people might throw tomatoes at you for no reason—just because she wanted to spend more time with Suprema. She wanted to ask Ruth if she missed her home, if she had family there, and if Abby was a terrible person because she had been thinking less and less about how much she missed hers, but she couldn't bring herself to say any of it. However, Ruth followed her silent line of questioning.

"You've got to do what feels right for you, okay? You want to be here; we'll find a way to make sure you stay. You want to go home; we can make that happen too. We don't got much, but we've all got each other, you know?"

There was a trust and assurance in her voice that Abby recognized. She had heard it before from Mr. Lambrinos, but she didn't believe it any more now than she had then. How could she believe that these people were *her* people? That they would help her and welcome her as one of them? After all, she had grown up in a home full of people who said they would look after her and keep her safe, but where were they now? Nonna had been ready to push her into Frank's arms, even knowing he treated her badly. Natale had fallen off the face of the earth. Words were nothing more than words until they were put to the test.

Suprema made her entrance third, just as she had said. What she had not mentioned was that, as she did so, a recorded lion roared offstage. She carried a rock, and while most of the crowd applauded, one voice louder than all the others called out, "It's fake! That's not a real rock!"

A rush of defensiveness overtook Abby. She wanted to jump to her feet and rush at the heckler. Ruth gripped her wrist. She didn't say a word, but Abby knew well enough what she meant.

Suprema dropped the rock, and it hit the stage platform with a loud thunk. Abby was certain it was about to crash on through to the ground. She then picked up a set of barbells, hoisted them into the air, tossed them lightly, and then caught them again. The audience cheered, except that same heckling voice that shouted, "Oh, come on, there's no way it's real."

Ruth gripped Abby's wrist all the tighter.

"You want to give it a try then? Or, I suppose, you would like me to lift you?" Suprema asked of the heckler, setting the barbell aside.

Ruth cringed. "Bad move."

Worried, Abby glanced at her, but didn't know what to say. She turned her attention back to Suprema, hoping that nothing was about to go wrong. Acknowledgment must have quieted the heckler, because no answer came.

"I thought not." She went back to the barbell and lifted it once again with one arm, then the other. Finally, she held it between both hands and, as Abby had seen her do at the athletic show, broke the metal rod holding the weights together in half.

The audience broke into thunderous applause. Abby jumped to her feet to give a standing ovation. Just as she was exiting, Suprema caught her eye and blew her a kiss. A shiver ran the length of Abby's body. A simple, but quite splendid, shiver.

After the show, Ruth took Abby by the hand and led her behind the tent. She marveled at how Ruth seemed drawn to Constance like iron to a magnet. They needed to be near each other. Abby did not feel that way, not even when Suprema came into view. She didn't gravitate toward her as though some desperate need to be whole could only be filled when she was near, and that didn't seem wrong. The lack of obsessive need made her attraction seem all the more right. When she saw her, she felt freer, more herself, more able to fly—something she had been missing for much longer than she had realized.

When she saw Suprema, she grinned broadly, then rushed forward to give her a hug. Suprema seemed taken aback. She hesitated for the briefest of moments, but before Abby could pull away, wondering if she had gone too far, she melted into Abby's arms, wrapping her own strong ones around her.

Abby could hear Suprema's heart and she rested her head against her. The difference in their heights was exacerbated by the brilliant red pumps Suprema wore. Suprema's heartbeat was quick and a little erratic, and Abby wondered if a high from performing or their current closeness was to blame. She couldn't hear her own heartbeats, but she could feel the heady, slightly dizzying sensation they were giving her.

"You were marvelous," she whispered, pulling back and taking Suprema's hands in hers. She was not ready to let go just yet, but was well aware of how public and exposed they were.

Suprema scoffed, shaking her head.

"Don't start," Abby replied, sensing the self-deprecation. "You were."

Thomas rushed toward them from the side of the tent.

"Abby Amaro!" he called out three times before she realized that he was calling her name. The other girls snickered, but Abby didn't mind. Practically panting, he came toward the group. "I've been looking for you everywhere."

"What is it, Thomas?" Abby asked, as a sense of apprehension rose.

"You've been so desperate for mail, I just figured ..." he trailed off, holding out a letter.

Abby gripped the letter in both hands. None of them breathed. They knew how much a letter from home meant to Abby. "There's no return address," she whispered, still afraid to open it. Warning lights were beginning to flash in her mind. What if the letter were from Frank? What if he had tracked her down?

"I'm sure it's from your brother," Ruth said with more urging than confidence in her voice.

Her hands trembling, Abby slid her index finger under the back flap and took out the pale pink perfumed stationery. This was certainly not from Frank, but it was unlikely to be from Natale either, and she doubted that her sisters would have a luxury like this paper. She unfolded it to find the name Mrs. M. Holland, along with the return address that had been missing from the envelope, embossed at the top of the page and neat, but elaborate, handwriting beneath.

Abigail,

Your letter startled me. I have not heard from a single one of you since that unpleasant business with my sister and I assumed that would remain the case in perpetuity. I am quite surprised, but pleased to have heard from you and doubly so to hear that you will be visiting my own home city this week. After a great deal of consideration, I have decided that I would, in fact, like to meet with you.

Now, we cannot meet at our new townhouse. Matthew has quite the nervous disposition about what the neighbors may think of us based on our choice of guests. Perhaps you would enjoy meeting at the aquarium. It seems like a nice and neutral place for the setting aside of grievances if there ever was any. This is not to say that I hold anything against you, dearest Abigail. It is simply my hope that you feel similarly towards me.

The best day for me to meet with you is Sunday afternoon when Matthew will be lunching with his mother. I shall wear my purple hat. You once mentioned that you were fond of it. Perhaps I shall give it to you. I rarely have cause to wear something as ostentatious any more.

My best regards,
Therese Holland

"Therese?" Abby muttered to herself, a bit put off by the stilted tone of her aunt's letter and the fact that she had altered the pronunciation of her first name. It was odd, but she was happy to have received a reply.

"What is it?" Suprema asked; her eyes showed concern. Abby wondered if her own expression betrayed her confusion.

"It's no—" Abby began to say, but then stopped herself. It was indeed something. She just wasn't sure what. "My aunt would like to meet with me is all, and I'm not sure that I want to."

Ah." Suprema nodded and slipped her hand into Abby's. Her expression still showed concern, but, as Abby said nothing more on the matter, she seemed unwilling to press it.

Constance clapped her hands. "We should get dinner!"

Ruth nodded. "And another dress for Abby, but after dinner. I want to see how the food tent reacts to her."

Abby glanced up at Suprema who looked back at her, her eyebrows raised with concern. "I'm going to be okay," Abby tried to say with her eyes, but Suprema's expression didn't change. A hurt was hidden there that Abby sensed had nothing to do with her.

Chapter Fifteen

A bouquet of roses lay outside Della's trailer when Abby arrived there that evening. They seemed to be casually discarded as opposed to carefully placed the way Thomas would have delivered them. That should have been a sign of things to come, but Abby was far too distracted by the day's emotions, both good and bad, to notice. She simply picked up the roses and walked inside.

Thanks to the lot's smell, all the trailer's windows had been kept closed; the slightest opening anywhere was stuffed full of scrap fabric. It gave the place a heavy, humid atmosphere. Abby sighed and set the roses on the table. It was too hot to stay in the trailer. "Someone sent you roses," she said, turning to go.

"They're not mine," Della said gruffly, climbing, barely dressed, out of the sleeping compartment and pulling the curtains tightly closed behind her.

"Someone sent you roses?" a groggy male voice echoed from her compartment. Abby stopped in her tracks.

"Again, they're not mine," Della repeated, this time to the sleeping compartment, sounding even more annoyed.

"Della, who do you—?"

"Is there someone here?" the male voice asked. "Are you trying to pull something freaky on me, Adelaide?"

Abby raised her eyebrows at Della, trying to say without words that she was not comfortable with this turn of events.

"Is this what you burlesque carnival girls get up to?"

"Della, get rid of him," Abby hissed.

"I'll get rid of who I want to," Della hissed back. Still, she threw open the curtains and snarled at the man there, who was dressed in nothing but his undergarments. He grinned up at her, but Della's rage was a sight to behold. If Abby hadn't known better, she would have sworn that every blonde hair on her head stood up and became a snake poised to attack. "*Get out!*" she bellowed. The man did not have to be told twice.

Della shut the door tight and latched it, then threw herself into a chair with a pronounced sigh. "All right, he's gone then."

"I'm sorry, if I had known—"

"Not necessary. Gave me an excuse to be rid of him. He was a bit of a square. Gave me these though." She plucked the large faux-pearl starburst earrings from her ears and set them down on the table next to the roses. Abby wasn't sure that was wise. They would probably be lost under a pile of fabric before long, never to be seen again. "'Sides, you're just riled 'cause it wasn't your brother. You sure these roses didn't have a note?"

Abby shook her head. She saw a man's suit jacket sleeve dangling out of Della's sleeping compartment. "Della, he forgot his jacket." She reached in to pick it up and stopped, seeing a slip of paper with very recognizable handwriting, Natale's handwriting.

"Maybe they're from your Amazon lady lover."

The sarcastic way she emphasized the word Amazon made Abby's blood boil. She grabbed the paper and spun around. "Don't you talk about her like that!"

"So it is true?" Abby was sure that if Della were a wild animal, she would have been baring her teeth. "You're seeing the Queen of the Jungle?"

"She has a name."

"Yeah, and do you know it?"

"Yes. S—"

"Don't you say Suprema. That's her bullshit stage name. It's no more her real name than mine is Miss Adelaide."

"Suprema is what she called herself to me, and if she wants something different, she can tell me herself." With great care and deference, Abby took the roses from the table and cradled them in her arms. She knew they couldn't be from Suprema. When would she have ordered them? Still, it was nice to pretend. They were a lovely dark red, almost the color of a glass of merlot—one of Abby's favorite colors. She took a deep breath, trying to hold on to the fragrance.

Della wrenched the roses from her arms with such force that Abby reeled backward.

"What are you doing?" Abby called out. "What's gotten into you?"

"They're mine, you idiot!" she said, putting them back on the table. "I was just pulling your chain, but you look like you're in love with that bitch."

Abby felt as though she had been slapped. She frowned, still clutching the note in her left hand.

"Are you?" Della asked, her eyes narrowing into an inscrutable expression.

Though she herself wasn't sure of the answer, defensive anger rushed her forward. "So what if I was?"

"I don't have a problem with her being a girl if that's what you're getting snippy about," Della said, sounding rather snippy herself. "I just think you're diving headlong into another batch of trouble. Natale asked me to look after you. You don't even know her!"

"I don't need you to protect me, Della. And besides, how is what I do any of Natale's business? He hasn't bothered to contact me, even though he knew how desperate I was to know everyone was okay. Not a single word. He won't even answer the phone, but he's writing love letters to you?" She hurled the note from her hands and onto the table.

The trailer was too hot for an argument. Both of them knew that, but they couldn't help themselves. Once the fight had begun, there was no stopping it. Della clenched her hands. "God, Abby, listen to yourself. You ran away with us to escape all this mucked-up love nonsense, and believe me, it is *all* mucked up, Abby. Deep down, I think you know that as much as I do. Nate's told me a bit about your family, and—"

"What's he been telling you about us?" Abby grabbed the letter and stopped cold. She could plainly see the date at the top right-hand corner. The letter was almost two weeks old, but then she saw another word. The salutation. The name was not Della, but Abby. Her tone as cold as ice, she asked, "What the hell is this?"

Della looked horror-struck, but did not say a word.

"This letter is for me?"

"I can explain," Della began. Abby was not in the mood to be placated. She wanted to rip Della's throat out, and not doing that was taking all of her energy.

"What is the matter with you? I know you don't want me here. Why not let Natale come and get me so I can go home?"

"You sure you want to go home now that you've got your woman?"

"Do not bring her into this!"

"Cut the gas, Abby, and listen to me for once!" Della began to pace. She tugged at her hair, looking frantic and desperate. "You wanna get all wrapped up in some kind of business that'll get you put away the second you step off this carnival lot, that isn't my business. Hell, I thought your awful personality was because you were some prude, but now I see the truth. You're sick in the head."

Her eyes stung. Della's words were too much. "Just because I don't have a different boyfriend in every town—you know, I have no idea what Natale sees in you. He can do so much better than some little tramp."

Della threw the bouquet of roses as hard as she could at Abby. "You have no idea what you're talking about! You think you know me?! No one could know me less than you!"

Abby was stunned. She wasn't the only one crying. Tears were falling from Della's carefully lined eyes. She had wanted to hurt Della back, but seeing the reaction was too much for Abby. She tried to take a step toward her, but Della swatted her away. "Della, I—"

"No," she said, taking a step back. "I need you to cut out of here. I need you to go."

"Go where?"

"I don't care. Just get out of my trailer. It's not like you've been a very productive seamstress anyway."

Abby didn't know how to respond. She stared at Della, who kept turning her face to hide the now-streaming tears. "Della, I'm sorry for whatever I—"

"I said, *get out!*" Her scream echoed in the tiny aluminum trailer. It sounded as if, in her anger and hurt, Della had split herself into hundreds of Dellas all bent on Abby's destruction. Abby ran out the door.

She hurried through the carnival lot, unsure where to go. She started in one direction, then another, then changed her mind again and found herself getting nowhere. She glanced back at Della's trailer, but she had switched off the lights already. There was no going back there tonight. Maybe in the morning, but not tonight.

Taking a deep breath, she started toward Suprema's trailer. Her heart started pounding at the thought of seeing her again. Della's words echoed through her mind. But she hadn't meant for any of this to happen. She was supposed to wait, patiently, until her brother came. She wasn't supposed to feel attraction for anyone. She wasn't supposed to want to stay. This life wasn't for her. She needed to go home and clear her head. If she could get her place back at the Music Institute, or even just her job at the diner, she could be the person she expected herself to be, the person everyone expected her to be. She didn't need a new romance. Romance only brought trouble and heartache.

~February, 1953~

Papa sits in the corner of the church social hall. He does not greet a single soul that approaches. He stares, but he does not see. Nonna stands behind him with a nervous hand on her son's shoulder. She looks as worried as Abby feels, but Abby tries not to show her concern as she leans against the door and watches the funeral reception come to an end. Her eyes are on her father as people file by and shake his hand. She doesn't hear their words, but she knows what they are saying: "I am so sorry for your loss." She's heard that too many times today, herself. It's one of the few things about the entire day that isn't a blur.

"Has he said anything?" Natale asks, walking up behind her.

Abby shakes her head. "Not a word. He doesn't even nod."

Natale sighs. "Have you seen Za Teresa? She was supposed to come take care of the little ones—"

Again, Abby shakes her head. "I'll go look after them. You call her. Maybe there's snow, and she couldn't get out."

Natale looks skeptical, but Abby doesn't want to think about it. She slips into the coatroom where her younger siblings have been squirrelled away. They don't know what is happening. None of them. Maybe Leon, who holds baby Annette and stares defiantly at the others, but Abby can't imagine even he fully grasps that their mother is gone. Not yet.

"Hey guys, who's hungry?" she asks, wobbly on her feet. They frown up at her, all except baby Annette who fusses and grabs hold of Leon's finger. He scowls. "Come on. Everybody out there means well."

"That bitch!" Natale's scream echoes down the corridor and into the room. Abby looks out the door, eyes wide. Her brother is not usually one for such language.

She takes a deep breath and rushes to the phone nook. He is standing there, still holding the receiver, while an unknown woman's voice on the other end of the line says, "Sir, your party has been disconnected; would you like me to try again?"

"Natale?"

"She's not coming. She's worried her fiancé will be scared off by her family. Apparently he has money. And apparently that's more important." He slams the receiver down as the operator once again tries to remind him of her presence on the line.

Abby touches his arm and shakes her head. "We don't need her anyway. We've got each other, right?"

Chapter Sixteen

Abby,

I don't know what to say. Normally, I'm better with words than this. I've written about a hundred letters in the past week to the most far-flung people in our family, and none of those letters were even half as hard to write as this one.

Abby, Nonna has passed.

There I wrote it. It's out there. You now know.

You should have been here, Abby. It is mean of me to put it that way, but I won't mince my words right now. You should have been here. Facing this alone was much harder than I expected it to be. Papa is as he's been, worse even. The kids are hurting. Carla won't leave her room. Annette walks around asking where Nonna's gone, and I don't know what to tell her. She was a baby when Mama died. She doesn't understand any of this. Leon's getting into fights, and Joseph is so quiet sometimes I wonder if he's forgotten how to speak.

The funeral is in two days. I know you won't be able to make it back in time and I can't ask you to, even though I need you here more than anything. It's not because of anyone here that I won't ask you. You have to do what's right for you. It's what Nonna wanted. She told me so. And, what Mama would have wanted, what I want. There will always be a place for you here. I need you, but I want you to do what you need to do.

Amuri,
Natale

Natale's words burned in her mind as she made her way through the unknown streets. "You should have been here." She could hear his voice and see his face as plain as day. Natale didn't ask for help. He looked out for her. He truly did need her, and no matter how many reasons she had for not wanting to go back—her fear of Frank, her desire to find out what there was between her and Suprema, her enjoyment of the carnival—if Natale needed her, she needed to go home to him.

Then her brain spun through the words again, settling on why he needed her: "Nonna has passed."

Nonna Gaetana, Abby's rock since childhood, had passed.

How was that possible? She had been so healthy. Sure, her mind had taken a hit or two. She repeated stories. She forgot people's names. Once or twice she spoke as though she were still a young woman in Sicily, or wrote letters to dead relatives. But she was healthy. Abby couldn't process how the world could suddenly not contain Nonna Gaetana. It seemed as though the world had always had her in it. How could her life just stop?

This wasn't the first death Abby had known, of course, but her mother had been growing frailer for years. Her mother had gathered her to her chest and whispered her goodbyes, her hopes, her dreams. They had parted knowing what was to come, knowing their love for each other. They had had closure. This, this was different.

Unwelcome tears streaming from her eyes, she made her way to the first pay phone she could find and flipped furiously through the phone book to the name Holland. There were at least ten "Holland, M"s on the page, but only one on the correct street. Abby took a deep breath, tried to choke back the tears so that should could sound poised, and then dialed.

"Holland Residence, this is Therese," said the airy voice on the other end of the line. Abby knew exactly what kind of training created that voice; plenty of the girls in her voice classes had been instructed in it. The person who answered was hiding an accent, and that fact was clear as day to someone who knew how to listen for it.

"Aunt Teresa, it's Abby. Ninfa's little girl."

"You sound just like her." The airy quality slipped just a hair. "Why are you calling? I agreed to meet you at the aquarium—"

"Something's come up. I need to get back to Cleveland as soon as possible."

"And you need money." Any hint of warmth in the fake voice was gone.

"No, it's not that. I mean, I would need to get a ticket back, but it's because I still—"

"You're more like your father than your mother. That's for sure."

Abby wasn't in the mood to think about what her aunt might have meant by this. "Can you meet me at the train station?" She really wanted to ask if she could stay with her aunt for the night, and they could drive back to Cleveland together in the morning, but she knew this was a pipe dream.

A long pause followed, and Abby wondered if her aunt had hung up the phone. She sighed, about to hang up, when Teresa finally responded in a whisper. "No. I cannot come, but I will send our maid to meet you with the fare for Ninfa's sake. You'll want the Englewood station. Lake Shore line, New York Central should be the fastest route. Give her at least an hour, maybe longer."

The words stung, but Abby accepted them for what they were. She was already flipping to the maps, looking for the train station and hoping it would not take too long to walk. "It will probably take me that long as well."

Using the maps torn from the pay phone directory, Abby made her way through the unfamiliar city streets. Chicago held a sense of foreboding vastness that Cleveland did not. She shrank from every person she passed as she pushed through the crowds, convinced they were all staring at her. Though she knew deep down this wasn't true, and that these people probably didn't give her a second thought, she couldn't shake the feeling; she had managed to convince herself that she was being followed, though she never saw anyone who stuck out when she turned around.

With a feeling of immense trepidation, she waited, eying the ticket counter. Every time someone stepped up to it, Abby's stomach clenched. Countless questions and anxieties raced through her head: What if her aunt's maid didn't make it in time? What if the train filled up? She held her hands tightly in her lap to keep them still, despite her trembling. She knew it was making people look at her, and that was the last thing she wanted. She wanted her aunt. She wanted to leave. She wanted—

"Can I get a cookie?" a small voice asked from next to Abby's elbow. For a split second, Abby believed that it was her own voice, an echo calling out from her last trip to Chicago to see Aunt Teresa. Then she looked. The voice belonged to none other than Phebe. "There's a man with a cart over there. He has coffee, too. Please?"

Abby gasped. "Phebe?! What are you doing here?"

"I came with you," she answered as though this were plain as day. "It's boring in the trailer, and I was just walking around the carnival and … I heard you say you were going to Cleveland." She looked at the floor of the station; her eyes trailed over each miniscule detail in the tiling. "I came to stop you."

Abby continued to stare. She had no memory of Phebe walking with her. "Why didn't you say anything until now?"

The little girl shrugged, still staring at the floor tiles and not making eye contact. "I… I was waiting for the right moment."

Shaking her head, Abby pulled the small girl into a hug. She was clearly upset, though Abby couldn't imagine why. "Phebe, this is silly. My home isn't here with the carnival. It's with my family."

"That's not true. They abandoned you like my family abandoned me."

Abby dearly wanted to ask what had given her such an idea, but years of similar conversations with her younger siblings, especially Annette, on the question of their mother, stopped her. "We have to get you home. Ruth and Constance are going to be worried. You're far too young to be wandering around Chicago by yourself."

"I'm with you. I'm fine."

"But I didn't know you were with me, Phebe. What if I'd gone somewhere that wasn't safe for you? And, Phebe, you really shouldn't be leaving the carnival; people can be—" she paused and glanced carefully around the station. If any eyes happened to peer in their direction, they turned away quickly. "Well, they can be cruel."

Phebe crossed her arms and looked at Abby with a fascinating mix of pout and glare that only an eight-year-old could ever master. "Can I just have a cookie?"

Abby met the expression head-on, narrowing her own eyes and trying to look stern, just as she would with Carla. "One. Then we're going right back to the carnival lot. Do you understand?"

Phebe nodded. "It smells there."

"Don't I know it?"

Abby made her way across the station to the old man with the coffee cart, glancing back toward Phebe every so often to make sure that she stayed on the bench and didn't wander off. "You wouldn't happen to have anisette for that coffee, would you?" Abby asked, examining the cart and picking up one of the sugar cookies, which were iced to look like fall leaves. Was autumn really upon them already?

The old man smiled, but shook his head. "I think I have some gin in this flask if you really need it."

"Thank you, but no." Abby took a few sticks of black licorice from one of the candy jars and dropped one into the paper coffee cup that the old man offered her. He wrinkled his nose. "I can pretend," she said, smiling, and gave him a few coins, which he took gratefully. Apparently, licorice in coffee wasn't so disgusting that he would mention it after she paid.

Phebe had waited patiently for Abby's return and took her cookie with a grateful smile. Abby sipped her coffee, which was too hot and had not sufficiently absorbed the licorice flavor, and watched Phebe from the corner of her eye before asking, "Phebe, how did you come to be at the carnival?"

Phebe swallowed politely before speaking. "I live with Ruth and Constance and Papa Lambrinos," she said, sounding somewhat rehearsed.

"Yes, but, you said you were abandoned?"

Phebe nibbled at the cookie and stared off into the gradually diminishing crowd in the train station. Abby waited patiently. "My mama put a note on my collar," she whispered after a minute or two of contemplative silence. "She left me at the sideshow. Constance doesn't think I know what it said, but I do. I told her I couldn't read it because I didn't want her to be sad for me."

"Oh, Phebe." Abby had expected something like this, but to hear it said in such a matter-of-fact, world-weary way from such a young child utterly broke her heart.

"Don't be sad. Ruth and Constance are better mothers anyway. They take good care of me." She nibbled on her cookie. It was obvious from the wrinkles on Phebe's brow that she had more on her mind. "Suprema will take good care of you."

Abby closed her eyes and inhaled slowly, then sipped her coffee. Phebe's mention of Suprema shook her like a bolt of lightning from a clear blue sky. She didn't know what she wanted or needed anymore. Not only was her brother's letter almost two weeks old, but another voice in her brain competed with her brother's written words. It belonged to Nonna Gaetana and repeated the last words that she had ever spoken to Abby: "Promise me you will never give in to what the world expects from you. Live the life that you want to live and be strong and never ashamed." She had promised her. Of course, at the time, she would have told her anything, whether or not it was true, just to make her proud, but now…

It wasn't just the thought of Suprema, but every opportunity that came with staying with her and the carnival. She was on the road now, just as she had always hoped to be. Sure, it was quite different from what she and Nonna had originally planned for her life, but when did things ever work out exactly as planned? She took one last sip of her coffee before tossing the cup into a nearby trash can. One final time, she glanced around for Aunt Teresa's maid. She had no idea what she might look like. But that didn't matter now. She didn't need train fare to Cleveland.

"Come on Phebe, let's go."

"You not leaving me after all?"

"No one is leaving anyone. Not today."

Abby brushed off a fly that had landed on her wrist and took Phebe by the hand. A cord connected the people of McClure's Amusements, and she was slowly beginning to understand how and why. They were outsiders, people who didn't belong to the wider society. This community sustained them and gave them something to rely on. Still, there was more than that, more than the desperation that comes from feeling alone in the world. These people were a true family. These people loved each other. Even Della, cold, haughty, vain Della, would move heaven and earth to keep Phebe safe when they were in Michigan.

Yes, there were fights. There were differences. There were cliques and people who weren't as close as they could be, but Abby knew that families tied by blood had those problems, too. Didn't Aunt Teresa prove that with her letter? The only thing she didn't know was whether or not she was part of the carnival family, whether or not those ties of love extended to her. She was starting to believe that she needed them more than ever.

Chapter Seventeen

THE CARNIVAL LOT SMELLED WORSE when Abby and Phebe returned because there was very little else to temper it. Except for a few straggling trucks and trailers, the lot was empty. The tents were down, the rides were disassembled, and most of the caravan had cleared out. It was hard to tell exactly what was left, since many of the light poles had been removed and the lot was rapidly growing darker as the sun set. Phebe gasped and looked up at Abby with panic in her eyes.

Abby didn't know what had happened. "Where is everything?" she asked.

"The jump," Phebe whispered, her lower lip shaking.

"They left?" Abby couldn't believe it. Sure the lot wasn't ideal, what with the distinct smell and all, but business was still decently brisk. There was no way they weren't going to finish out the week in a city as big as Chicago, unless something awful had happened. Beyond that, Abby couldn't fathom why they had all left in just a few hours. What had occurred must have been dire. "How could they have left?"

Phebe sobbed. Tears streamed down her face, and the only sounds she made were small heart-wrenching gasps for air as she clutched her arms tightly around her chest.

"Come on, Phebe, don't cry. There—there's still some people here. Let's go find out what's happening."

This only seemed to make her sob harder.

Abby gathered her close, trying to hold on to her the way she had seen Ruth do from time to time. "Come on now, Phebe, come on." When Phebe continued to cry, Abby lifted her into her arms. She was a bit too big for Abby to lift properly, but Abby gritted her teeth and started toward the first truck she could see.

She passed by the first and the second, not recognizing them and getting an odd feeling from the glares they gave her and Phebe. Pushing her way on through the empty field, she finally saw a familiar face, but it was one she wanted nothing to do with: Gregor was rushing toward them at breakneck speed.

"You found her!" he cried, his expression changing from frantic to relieved.

"I—" Abby had carefully avoided Gregor since day one. Even when she had been trying her hand at the sideshow bally, she hadn't looked him in the eyes, and he had seemed to agree with this arrangement. Now, however, he rushed toward Abby and gathered her and Phebe into a hug. Abby couldn't help freezing.

"Sorry," he said, backing away immediately. "I just—God, you must know how a father can be when a child is lost ..." he trailed off, glancing at the beat-up truck and small trailer in the field behind him. Abby couldn't see anyone else in it, but she could only assume his family was inside, waiting.

"What happened?" Abby managed to force out.

Gregor shook his head. "No one is quite sure. The word came down that we were out of here by midnight. Most have already left."

"But why?"

Squeezing Phebe's hand once more, Gregor backed away with a shrug. "I can only assume some sort of scuffle. Probably police, but possibly locals. I wasn't told, but there have been many rumors, some of a raid. That scares people. We can all move very quickly when needed, as you know."

Abby's heart sank as she ran through her options. Her ride, Della, was probably long gone. She didn't see anyone else she knew. She could either go back to the train station in the hope that her aunt's maid had waited there, or she could ask Gregor for a ride to the next town. "Gregor," she began, trying to calm her nerves, which were racing under her skin.

He raised an eyebrow, urging her to go on, but she couldn't. She stared sheepishly, afraid of the answer.

But she didn't have to ask. Another voice broke through the gathering darkness. "Phebe! Phebe, where have you been?!" Constance ran to her and gathered her into her arms. Phebe began crying anew, but these tears seemed to be tears of relief.

"You didn't leave me?" she asked, her voice still small and more frightened than Abby had heard it.

"Of course not!" Constance closed her eyes. Her face seemed to clear of a terror Abby fully understood. "How could you think that?"

Phebe didn't answer. She just clung to Constance as if she would disappear at any moment.

Tears were also streaming from Constance's eyes. She was usually so put together; Abby was quite shocked to see them. "Thank you for finding her," Constance said, pressing her face against Phebe's.

Abby knew that expression well. Her own mother had worn it from time to time: when Joseph fell from his bike, when Carla had a fever. It was a look that said, "Everything will be all right" and "Thank God, you're okay" simultaneously. She took a step back, watching the pair of them, the tiny family, and felt a hollowness in her heart. Did she make the right decision at the train station? She had no way of knowing. She had brought Phebe back to where she belonged. She had brought about this moment, but she missed her own family now more than ever. Would that ache ever abate now that Nonna Gaetana was gone?

"Constance?" Abby asked gingerly when she heard the sputter of Gregor's trailer engine come to life.

"Della's gone," Constance answered, not taking her eyes from Phebe. "But if you need a ride I can think of someone still hanging around who would be more than happy to take you."

As the three of them made their way back into the lot, Abby could see that there were still a number of trailers not yet ready to be moved. The Lambrinos's was one of them. Ruth stood out front, pacing and staring out into the darkness. Her face looked paler than ever, and she resembled a sentry on the night before a battle.

When they came into view, however, her face cleared and she rushed forward just as Constance had. "Don't you ever do that to me again," she whispered fiercely, pulling Phebe into a tight hug.

Phebe squirmed but hugged her back. "Abby found her," Constance said.

Ruth sighed. She still looked somewhat shaken as she led Phebe back to the trailer. "I'll make some hot cocoa; I think all of us need it."

"I had coffee an hour or so ago, I don't need—" But Ruth's expression brooked no argument. She followed the family inside.

Abby waited as Constance prepped the cocoa and Ruth fussed over Phebe. She smiled to herself, though her heart ached just a little. She was about to attempt to excuse herself when a rap came at the trailer door.

"We're about to go!" Constance called out.

The door opened. Boleslaw, looking quite presentable in his best suit, stood there. His face was creased and worn with worry, and he seemed decades older. "Phebe!" he said. Abby recognized the pain deeply hidden in his voice. He had lost people before. "You found her then, I assume?"

"We did," Constance answered.

Boleslaw glanced around the trailer. When his eyes settled upon Phebe, curled up asleep in Ruth's lap, his entire appearance seemed to change. Years lifted from his face, and he was himself again. "Thank the Lord," he said, breathlessly. "We were all terrified. None more than you, I'm sure."

Constance put a hand on Ruth's arm. They nodded as one.

"I'll let you get settled then." He turned to go, then stopped, seeming to notice something. "Miss Amaro?"

Abby nodded sheepishly.

"I thought you'd gone home to your family."

Not wanting to get into the details of the story now, if ever, she shook her head. "No, I just decided not to ride with Della for now."

Boleslaw nodded, but his eyes were narrowed. "When Miss Adamson told me you would be leaving, I had assumed she meant leaving the show altogether."

"No," Abby said, watching him. He hadn't moved from the doorway, and she could not squeeze past him without seeming rude, but she desperately wanted to locate Suprema before she left the lot.

"Beverly will be pleased." A playful smile appeared briefly on his lips. It reminded her of the day she first saw him. Abby couldn't help the blush that crept over her face. "Miss Constance, please let Alejo know that I will speak with him once we arrive in Kokomo."

"I will."

He slipped out then, giving Abby the perfect chance to escape. She only hoped that she wouldn't be too late.

Chapter Eighteen

Her heart pounded as she knocked upon the closed and darkened trailer, feeling all the more exposed and ridiculous with each bang of her fist against the aluminum.

Just as she was about to go, hoping that the Lambrinos family had not yet begun the jump, she heard a creak. A light clicked on, and she heard the turn of a bolt. Suprema opened the door. Ashen-faced and wide-eyed when she saw Abby standing before her, she said, "You didn't leave?" Her voice was hesitant, almost frightened, as if part of her expected to be speaking with a hallucination.

"I thought about it, but … I changed my mind."

Suprema didn't step closer. It seemed as though the doorway between them was a mile-wide barrier. "I thought you'd gone," she said solemnly. "I thought maybe I'd scared you away."

"No. It's not you," Abby said, though that wasn't entirely true. She didn't want to explain why; she just wanted to be held. "It was nothing about you. I was a little scared, but not because of you." She moved forward, crossing the distance between them. Suprema wrapped her arms around her and held her gently as tears slipped unbidden from her eyes.

"Abby—"

"I need to cry," she said between her sobs. "I'm so sad. Why can't I cry?"

"You are crying," Suprema whispered, still holding her as if she were a china doll.

"I never even told her where I was. I should have just sent the letter. Even if it was full of lies. At least she would have thought I was singing. She wanted me to be a singer, or get married, now—now she won't get to see either."

Suprema didn't answer. She held on to Abby as she cried. Then, once again, Nonna Gaetana's words came into Abby's mind. This time they were crisper, more demanding, than they had been on the day she said them. "Promise me you will never give in to what the world expects from you. Live the life that you want to live and be strong and never ashamed." No, Nonna Gaetana didn't just want her to be a singer or get married; she wanted her to be happy.

"I had wanted to talk about, you know, this," Suprema started. "Well, but maybe now isn't …"

Each of them considered the other. Abby looked into Suprema's eyes, as her own still shone with tears. She didn't know what it would take to live up to her promise to Nonna Gaetana. She didn't know what she wanted from life or how to make herself happy. What she could do now was find out what Suprema had to say. "Now is exactly the time."

Suprema pulled away and took Abby by the hand. With a gentle tug, she led her into the trailer and latched the door.

"Aren't we supposed to be leaving?" Abby asked. The prospect of being left behind once again opened a pit in her stomach.

Suprema shook her head, scanning the slowly emptying lot from her window. "Can't go anywhere until my uncle hooks the Empire up to his truck. We're always the last to leave."

"He seems pretty busy."

"Yeah, the whole thing's a mess. Someone has been spreading rumors about the carnival harboring communist spies. I don't know where they get these things. And, his health, he is in no shape to be dealing with all of this. I worry about him." Suprema took a seat and gestured for Abby to join her. "But he's proud of what he's done and way too proud to step down. I mean," she glanced at Abby, who still hadn't sat down, and sighed. "The human blockhead act is impressive. He's one of the best, but I'm fondest of other stuff that he's done. For example, getting me out of that hellhole I lived in."

Abby still couldn't bring herself to sit. Instead, she leaned against the trailer's small table and watched Suprema's face as she spoke. In the background, her radio hummed quietly: an old, jazzy Sinatra tune, the kind her mother was always enamored with.

"My family's very different from yours, Abby."

"You don't know that," Abby began, a little apprehensive that Suprema might be making assumptions about her.

"No, you're right, but you seem to love them. Not hearing from them bothers you, so, that's something."

Abby nodded. "I suppose that's true."

"Here, let me show you something." Suprema went to the drawer beneath her sleeping compartment and pulled out a small box, which she brought to the table. Once again, she gestured for Abby to sit, and this time she did. Suprema carefully removed several mementos: a few faded hair ribbons, a tarnished silver ring, and a tiny bird whistle. Underneath were several photographs. Suprema laid one before her, showing an older, but well-kept, house that reminded Abby a lot of her own neighborhood back on Murray Hill Road. In front of it stood a family of three: a tall gentleman, who looked like a younger version of Boleslaw; a squat woman with her hair tied up under a shawl; and between them, a surly, almost-teenaged Suprema. She looked nothing like she did now. Her hair was tied back in pigtails with long ribbons and she wore a dress so ruffled that Abby almost found it comical. Still, her face gave her away.

"Is this you?" Abby asked.

"I want you to know that I understand. I want you to know all the parts of me, even the messy parts. This is the messiest part, and this is the only way I can explain it." Her face was a blank mask. Abby couldn't read even a hint of emotion on it. Still, she knew that something was hidden beneath the surface. Perhaps a horrible memory. Perhaps a lovely one, sorely missed.

"You don't have to talk about anything you're not ready to talk about."

Suprema shook her head. "You need to know. It tried to kill me. This house, these people, would have killed me if I let them." The words spilled out of Suprema's mouth faster than Abby could process them. "Not directly, of course. I mean, it's a house, but the things that happened here… If it hadn't been for Boleslaw…"

Abby held her hand and waited. She wasn't sure what to say.

"They said I was sick, that they would send me to a special doctor to fix the things that had gone wrong in my brain. If it hadn't been for Boleslaw," she said a second time. This time there was venom in her voice. She spat on the ground the way Nonna Gaetana used to do. "He got me out. Took me to the carnival instead."

"They?" Abby still didn't know what to say. It was as if she were walking along the edge of a cliff, and one wrong move would send her right over the edge.

Suprema nodded. "My parents. When they saw me kiss… Helen… her name was Helen."

Abby swallowed hard.

She picked up the bird whistle and handed it to Abby. "She gave me this. I was thirteen. She was pretty. I don't know why I'm telling you this…"

Abby squeezed Suprema's hand as if that one simple gesture could convey all the sympathy, protectiveness, and love she was feeling. Suprema squeezed back, and Abby felt warmth rush through her whole body.

"Thank you for telling me," Abby whispered.

"I thought you should know," Suprema replied, not looking at her. Abby could tell that her mind was years in the past with the frightened girl whose parents did not understand what she needed. "They weren't great before that, either, but I think it was something of a last straw for my uncle. He couldn't stand to see me hurting anymore. He and I, we don't always see eye to eye, about my act, about most things, but he loves me. Thanks to him, I have a real family."

"I didn't run away from you," Abby said, after letting what Suprema had said settle between them. "Della had kept a letter from me. It said that my grandmother passed away a few weeks ago, and, for a minute, I just needed to get home."

"I could have gone with you," Suprema offered.

Abby shook her head. "No. God, no. I couldn't. That's *way* too much to expect this early in a relationship."

"Relationship?" Suprema asked.

Abby blushed. She had said the word without realizing it, without fully meaning to, but there it was. She stopped cold, as did Suprema, who looked at her with confusion, but also with something akin to happiness. "I—"

"Do you mean that?"

"I want to."

"I don't know that I'll be good in a relationship," Suprema said after a moment of silence. "I've avoided it for so long."

"Neither do I," Abby said, and wanted to laugh as she said it. "My last relationship was so bad, and it was the only one I've ever had. I don't think I know what to do or how to be. I'm afraid of being hurt again."

"I can't make you any promises."

"My father once said that promises were for weak men to hide behind. The only thing we can do is live."

"Wise words," Suprema whispered.

Abby turned away and peered out of the blinds at the dark carnival lot. It looked eerie and empty, and her heart ached at the impenetrability of the darkness. She had the distinct sense that she was back on the haunted train ride where the strobe lights completely blocked out her vision. She had ridden this "relationship" ride before, and it hadn't ended well. The darkness of the future could mask any number of dangers, but maybe it could hide joy too.

Abby didn't have the words to explain. Instead she kissed Suprema. Suprema seemed frozen, and Abby pulled back, feeling awkward and out of line. "I'm so sorry," she said.

"Don't be," Suprema said, initiating a kiss of her own. This time, they kissed each other. It was tender and sweet, cautious but hopeful. There was a softness, and a depth, that Abby had not experienced before. Only their lips touched for the longest time. Then Abby touched Suprema's face. She needed something to ground her, something to make her believe that all this was for real. Gingerly, she trailed her fingertips along Suprema's exquisite jawline and then into her hair; a thrill ran through her.

Eventually, Suprema took Abby's hand, held it, and broke away from the kiss. Their faces remained close as they looked into each other's eyes. Again, Abby was mesmerized by the blue-gray of Suprema's eyes.

"Your eyes are so dark," Suprema whispered. "I could get lost in them."

"They're just a really dark shade of brown," Abby demurred.

"No, they're the forest at night."

"Well, yours are—" Abby couldn't think of a good way to phrase what she wanted to say. Instead, she moved forward and kissed her again. They had plenty of time before anyone came to hook up the trailer.

Chapter Nineteen

Natale,

I just received your letter. I suppose mail on the road can take time. More time than I would like. I wanted to call. I wanted to come home. I still do. I even tried to contact Za Teresa, but before you yell at me, I came to my senses. Nonna told me to find a way to be happy. It was the last promise I ever made her, Natale. Right now, the carnival is what makes me happy. I hope that you can understand and forgive me.

I will come home. Soon. When the season has ended. There are only a few stops left. I have so much to tell you and the little ones. I think of them often. I have enclosed some toys I got for them from the one of the games. Say I won them for them and that I will be home soon.

Amuri,
Abby

P.S. You should bring them out when we are in Urbana. I bet the kids would love a vacation.

Suprema laced her pinky finger through Abby's. The sweet, gentle gesture moved Abby more than she liked to admit. It was a simple thing, small, unassuming, but it sent a thrill through her every time, as if a connection had opened between them with just this one, almost unnoticeable, contact. A smile on her lips, she glanced over at Suprema.

"What?" Suprema asked, beginning to blush.

"Just looking at you."

Suprema blushed even more. Her complexion turned rosy. Abby took Suprema's whole hand, interlacing their fingers. The pickled punks tent had just emptied of Kokomo townies, and Abby had Suprema all to herself. The moment was sweet, even if they were surrounded by rubber aliens in jars.

"I wish the summer were longer," Abby whispered, trying not to sound as mournful as she felt.

"No, you don't."

"I feel like I've only gotten started. There's so much more I need to do."

Suprema didn't say anything. She simply squeezed Abby's hand reassuringly.

"Where do you go in the winter?" Abby asked after a silent moment had passed.

"I'm not a bird," Suprema said with a light laugh. Abby watched her face, the way her nose wrinkled just slightly. She was beginning to learn how the smallest variations in expression could indicate the biggest differences in feelings. Suprema blinked when she was sad and closed her eyes for long moments when she thought she was making others sad. Abby's favorite, an almost imperceptible twist of her lip, meant she was angling for a kiss. A wrinkled nose, though, from what Abby had gathered so far, meant she was deflecting. Suprema deflected in a number of ways. She lashed out at people she hadn't allowed into her circle, but she had other methods: sarcasm, humor, always a wrinkled nose. Abby was surprised no one else seemed to have noticed.

"No, but the Lambrinos family goes south, right?"

"Yeah, to Florida."

"And you? And your Uncle Boleslaw?"

Suprema closed her eyes. Abby waited for the blink. She felt bad for pushing. Sometimes she wasn't sure when to push and when to let a subject go. Suprema kept her eyes closed and squeezed Abby's hand. "We don't go to Florida," she said, still not opening her eyes. Abby nodded. Just as she was about to change the subject, Suprema spoke again. "We make camp with the McClures in Nashville."

"I was expecting somewhere that stayed warm all winter."

"Tennessee is warmer than Cleveland."

Abby laughed. That was true enough. "Lake effect snow," she said, trying to sound wistful and nostalgic, though that particular weather phenomenon was difficult to love.

"Blistering, minus-forty wind chills," Suprema said, mimicking her tone. Abby kissed her cheek, and Suprema lifted Abby's hand to her lips, where she left a lingering kiss that sent a chill down the entire length of Abby's spine.

"Why the sudden concern with winter?" Suprema asked, after savoring the moment of silence. "I thought you couldn't wait to get home to your family?"

Gnawing guilt snuck into Abby's stomach at Suprema's words. She had felt this guilt on and off. She wanted to go home, of course she did. That had been her goal ever since she set foot on the carnival lot the night of the athletic show. But she also was truly beginning to come into her own. She felt confident in her singing and even more in her day-to-day life. This trip was what she had needed, this chance to build something on her own. She was coming to realize that it was about to be snatched from her before she'd had the chance to realize its full potential.

"It's complicated," was all Abby found herself able to say.

"It's not me, is it?" Suprema asked, a hint of concern in her voice. "I mean, I don't want you to go, but I want you to do what's going to make you happy, and we haven't known each other all that long ..."

Abby shook her head as Suprema trailed off. "It's not you," she said with passionate sincerity. "I miss my family, but I want to be here. I think my being here, at the carnival, is right."

Suprema scrutinized her face, then broke into a smile. "You do fit, you know? I hope you know."

Abby appreciated those words more than she was willing to admit.

"I wonder if this is where they hid the Russian spies?" a young boy's voice hissed just outside of the tent.

"It says they're aliens, Billy, not Russians," a girl who sounded about the same age pronounced.

"Well, they can't very well put a sign up that they're Russians, now, can they, Rebecca?"

"Not this communist spies nonsense again," Suprema muttered as she and Abby laughed.

Abby held a finger to her lips and snuck as silently as possible to the tent's entrance.

"Are you saying that the carnival people lie to us?" Rebecca seemed not to believe in this possibility.

Billy, however, was more cynical. "Yes. They do it all the time, you know. I read about it."

Abby opened the tent. "Is someone looking for some aliens?"

The pair, neither of whom looked much older than five, both gasped. "A communist!" Rebecca cried out, and the two raced away as fast as their small feet could propel them. Abby couldn't help chuckling.

"Oh, now they're going to tell their parents." Suprema was laughing as well, but a twinge of guilt prickled Abby's spine.

"I didn't think," she said apologetically. "I used to scare my little brothers and sisters like that all the time."

Suprema waved a hand as if to dismiss Abby's concern. "Don't worry about it."

Abby felt the worry settle in her stomach like a rock. "I suppose I should get back to work, try to bally my red aliens." She tried to tease, but the joke sounded forced.

"Yeah, and they'll need me back on the ten-in-one." Suprema kissed her quickly before turning to go. "Meet me after. It's my last show of the day. We can have a drink before the athletic show."

The kiss goodbye was soft and perfect, and Abby felt warmth spread through her. She forgot about the guilt. She didn't even hear Suprema say the words, "athletic show."

AT THE BACK OF THE show tent, Abby found Boleslaw, Alejo Lambrinos, and Mrs. McClure in intense conference.

"We cannot just keep fleeing every time there is a whisper," Mr. Lambrinos said confidently.

"That's easy for you to say. They'll cart me off to hear me talk," Boleslaw protested.

"Now, now, Mr. Wolski," Mrs. McClure said, sounding so even-keel she could soothe the most anxious soul. She looked as poised as she ever had, but a small vein pulsed in her forehead. "People on the midway talk. We cannot stop them from doing so. This is not the same as Chicago, though. There, Thomas had concrete evidence that we were to be investigated. I personally found the whole matter silly, as we have nothing to hide, but who's to say what sort of things can be made to look a certain way in a certain light—"

"That's what I've been trying to say!" Mr. Wolski shouted.

"Miss Amaro!" Alejo interrupted. Boleslaw and Mrs. McClure stopped speaking and looked at her.

"Abby!" Mrs. McClure said, walking toward her, arms outstretched like a society woman who had just seen an old friend about to commit a faux pas. "Abby, I haven't seen you in some time. Della hasn't brought you by the girl show."

"No," Abby demurred, having no desire to discuss how things had fallen out with Della.

"I was hoping you could talk to her for me."

"Well, I—"

Before Abby could protest, Mrs. McClure had wrapped her arm around her shoulder and begun leading her away from the show tent. "Della is troubling me," she said as they walked. "Her act has been getting more and more dangerous. She has done double somersaults without rehearsal and attempted triples; it's as if she—" Mrs. McClure cut herself off and took a deep breath. "I care a great deal for her, Miss Amaro. I knew her mother well. I fear she is trying to harm herself. I do not know why. I tried to speak with her, but she will not listen to me; perhaps you can get through to her."

Abby frowned, remembering how dangerous Della's act had seemed with only one somersault. "I don't know, Mrs. McClure," she whispered. "Have you tried to talk to the other girls? Vivian?"

"Unfortunately, they had little information for me. I was hoping that since you are her traveling companion—"

"Not since Chicago," Abby admitted.

Mrs. McClure pursed her lips. "Oh, I was not informed." She studied Abby, then said flippantly, "Well, do you think you could get over your little spat so she stops trying to break her own neck?"

Abby could not speak. She stared at Mrs. McClure in stupefied silence. Then, when words finally returned, she shouted, "How dare you put that on me!"

"I didn't mean to imply—"

"Yes, you did." Abby shook Mrs. McClure's arm from her shoulder and stormed back to the show tent. Alejo and Boleslaw watched with wide eyes as she marched past them and slipped into the back without another word.

Chapter Twenty

"I CAN'T BELIEVE YOU TOLD off her highness McClure," an astonished Vinnie muttered as he sat down with Abby and Suprema at one of the beer garden's picnic tables.

"How did you hear about that?" Abby asked, panic rising in her throat. Suprema put a hand on her knee and gave it a squeeze, which helped, but didn't completely alleviate Abby's anxiety.

"Are you kidding? Everyone's talking about it. You're more interesting than speculating over whether or not we're gonna get run out of town for harboring communists again."

"Oh, God!" Abby dropped her head to the table and covered it with her arms.

"Vinnie," Suprema pleaded. "Be nice, please. She's really embarrassed."

"Hey, all of us have wanted to do it from time to time. Sofia can be a little... abrupt. It's probably why she gets on so well with your Della."

"I wish everyone would stop calling her my Della. It's not my job to keep her from being a nosebleed."

"What's she on about?" Vinnie asked.

Suprema sighed and gently touched Abby's hair. "Nothing, Vinnie."

"Look, pint-size," Vinnie voice was no longer teasing, but entreating. "Sorry. I didn't mean anything by it. I'll get the next round?"

When Abby still didn't lift her head, Suprema kissed the top of it. "We have to get going to the athletic show. Unless you're not feeling up for it."

"I can't. No," Abby said, lifting her head.

Suprema nodded her understanding. Abby hadn't told her that she had no interest in ever seeing an athletic show again, but she greatly appreciated the fact that Suprema hadn't pushed her. "Well, be ready for the jump after. Uncle B's raring to go."

"I will."

As Suprema disappeared into the crowd, Vinnie hummed. "Well, well, well, isn't that cute?"

"You writing a book or something?" Abby asked him with narrowed eyes.

"She's rubbing off on you already. That is something she'd say to *me*—has said to me, come to think of it, more than once."

"Vinnie…"

"Let me have this. It's not every day that something I set up actually works out. This would be the first time, in fact."

Abby shook her head. "It's new, okay, but it makes me happy."

"I'm glad, pint-size. I really am. I only tease because you blush."

"It's not like it was with Frank at all."

"From you've told me, that's a good thing." Vinnie took a long sip of his beer as he watched her.

"How do I know it won't end up the way it did with Frank?"

Vinnie shrugged. "Well, they weren't all like that, were they?"

"What all?" Abby asked with a laugh. "The only person I ever dated was Frank!"

Taking a long, deep breath, Vinnie sighed. "You can't think so many steps ahead all the time. That's how you end up like me. I ran from everyone because I thought they'd leave me like Gianni did, and now?"

Abby sighed. "I suppose you're right."

"If something makes you happy, it makes you happy. Experience it."

"I think I've heard that somewhere."

"Speaking of which, do you want to sing a folk song? I brought my accordion."

Abby glanced around furtively, blushing when she saw all the people milling about, but then she grinned.

The jump was long, and they did not arrive in the next town until well after three in the morning. Abby drifted in and out of sleep as they traveled. Her dreams were strange and unsettled. She dreamt of Della standing on a bridge, threatening to jump, and when Abby raced to stop her, a crowd of people said, "It's all your fault." She dreamt of everyone in the carnival from Mrs. McClure to Jimmy the haunted train ride operator being arrested and taken away for wearing red clothes at least once in their life. When her dream-self chased Suprema, she heard Frank saying, "Now, now, don't you think this all could have been avoided?" She woke shivering. The caravan had stopped, and it was time to get some real rest before setup. Abby didn't know if she could.

"Hey," Suprema whispered. "Are you all right?"

"I'm fine, I'm fine," Abby hissed, as Suprema got up and began digging in the storage area beneath the bed. "Please come back, it's cold without you."

Suprema raised an eyebrow. "Are you really that much of a romantic, or are you actually cold-blooded?"

Abby simply smirked at her sleepily. "Why don't you come back and find out?"

Suprema plugged in an electric blanket and pulled it over the two of them. It was small and required some strategic cuddling, but neither seemed to mind. Suprema kissed her neck as the warmth of the blanket kicked in, and Abby drifted off into a blissful sleep.

The next morning when Abby woke, she was alone in the trailer. The air, for the first time since she had joined the caravan, was crisp and bitter. Abby didn't want to brave the cold to find out what was being served in the food tent. Instead, she burrowed farther under the electric blanket, trying to feel warm again. She reached under her pillow where she had put Natale's letter for safekeeping and read over the words yet again. There was still no greater meaning in them, but the hollowness in her chest abated just seeing the name Natale Amaro in his handwriting. After her third reread, the door of the trailer creaked open. Suprema carried in two mugs of coffee, which she put down on the table next to the radio before glancing sheepishly at Abby.

"I thought you'd still be asleep," she said, seeming surprised to see Abby at all, let alone awake. "You didn't sleep well, did you?"

"I only just woke up." Abby watched her carefully, taking in each movement, even the way her hair fell, trying to commit it to memory in case what she had dreamed came to pass.

"I brought coffee," she said, nodding at the mugs. "And then, I have to ask you something."

Abby scrambled to the table, bringing the electric blanket with her, wrapped tightly around her shoulders like a cloak. "You're a coffee angel," she said, picked up the miraculously still piping hot mug, and took a sip. It burnt her tongue, but she had far bigger things on her mind. As Suprema sipped from her own mug, Abby wondered if it were cocoa. Suprema didn't strike her as the coffee-drinking type. "What was it you wanted to ask me?" she asked.

Suprema shook her head. "Not yet."

This puzzled Abby, but she nodded, waiting. The moment she had finished her coffee, Suprema took Abby by the hand. She kissed her sweetly on the cheek and, in a hesitant voice that Abby hadn't heard in a while, she asked, "Will you please tell me what you were dreaming about?"

Abby hesitated. "It was just a dream."

"You were crying in your sleep. I… I only want to understand. You don't have to."

"No, it's just… It's silly, I think."

"I like silly things," Suprema teased.

Abby smiled, remembering that she had tried to make the same joke on their pizza parlor date. "Fine." She went on to describe the choppy, disjointed dreams, and Suprema listened, her face a blank mask betraying no emotion. She looked almost analytical.

"My Aunt Ida," she explained, when Abby had finished, "used to interpret people's dreams. It was part of her act."

"Are you going to interpret mine?"

Suprema shook her head and took Abby's hand. "I don't know what dreams mean. I don't know if they mean anything, but if you're that worried about Della, we can go talk to her."

"Maybe."

"And we're not going to be arrested, you know. We're too good."

Abby moved closer to Suprema and allowed herself to be pulled into a warm embrace. She didn't want to think about her dreams right now.

~*September, 1942*~

ABBY PEEKS DOWN THE STAIRS from the landing. She has been told to stay in her room, but the men are so loud when they come in, and she can't sleep. Instead, she sneaks down the stairs. If she stands in just the right spot, she can see the kitchen, but no one in it will be able to see her. It's a great spot for spying on Mama and Nonna when they argue about the right way to prepare artichokes or drink anisette, even though neither of them would ever admit to Abby that they did that.

The men have scowls on their faces and are loud when they speak. They are not yelling, but Abby can sense they are close to it. She's heard this same tone of voice from many people, from her teacher when she threw a pencil at Jimmy Russo and her papa when she accidentally broke a fancy red vase that Nonno had brought from Sicily.

One of them leans on the kitchen table toward Mama and asks, "And where is your husband now, ma'am?"

Her mother, beautiful with her dark eyes, and darker curls tied up in a bandanna, sits poised and upright in a chair, sipping coffee from one of her special tiny cups. Two mugs sit on the table in front of her; they are steaming away, untouched. "You know well enough," she replies, keeping her composure in a way that frightens Abby. She only speaks this calmly when she is angry or afraid, as when Abby refuses to run errands or when she's talking about where Papa is or when he's coming back. "He is in the Pacific."

"Why the Pacific?"

"Because that is where he was sent."

"Why?"

"Because he's in the Navy. Do you honestly expect me to know?" She sips casually from her cup as Abby's heart beats wildly. She's afraid the sound of it will give away her hiding place. "Loose lips sink ships."

The man paces the length of the room. He looks back at her as if trying to pretend that a question had just occurred to him. "Ma'am, let me just ensure that my information is accurate. You are Italian?"

"That is correct."

"And are you naturalized?"

"Excuse me?" Mama asks without looking up from her coffee.

"Are you naturalized?" he repeats. Abby doesn't understand what the word means, but it seems to offend her mama.

Abby's mother inhales deeply of the steam from her coffee mug. As small as she is, Abby recognizes this gesture. This was a trouble-is-about-to-begin gesture, a steeling-herself gesture. She usually only does it before an argument with Nonna or before little Abby and Natale need to be disciplined. It makes Abby uncomfortable to see it now. Mama opens her eyes and meets the man's. "I suffered through that godforsaken island of yours, is that not enough for you?"

The two men exchange a glance. Then the second man drops a collection of envelopes on the table. "And can you explain these?"

Mama reaches for the envelopes. Her hands are still young and nimble. They have not yet grown weak from the disease that would take her ten years later. She carefully removes sheets of crisp white stationery from the envelopes and examines their contents. "Yes, these appear to be letters to my sister in Chicago. No wonder she seemed so perturbed on the telephone."

"Letters?" the man asks, his eyebrow raised. "And what do they say?"

Mama begins to read the letter in her hand. "Teresa, Spero—"

"English, please," the man interrupts.

She takes a deep breath and begins again. Abby notices that her words are slow and stilted as though masking an anger she wants to unleash on the man who is leaning on her brand-new table. "Teresa, I hope you are well. I struggle here as I am alone. I must find ways to pass my time. The children do not occupy me as they should—"

"That sounds coded."

"It's awkwardly worded, yes. It flows better in Italian."

The man ignores her. He takes another envelope off the table and roughly pulls out one of the papers. "And what is this?"

Mama blinks, turning the paper to examine the sequence of circles and dashes. After a moment, she begins to laugh. 'It's a knitting pattern," she says, her expression clearing. "All this trouble is about a knitting pattern?"

The men are not laughing. "Ma'am, this is serious," the one leaning on the table says.

"Yes, deadly serious. Lord knows what my sister would do with a pair of woolen stockings. She could take down the whole of Chicago."

The men exchange a glance and nod. "Ma'am, you are under arrest."

Color drains from Mama's face. She looks suddenly ill. "Excuse me?"

"You know well enough that an enemy alien such as yourself is not be caught in possession of, or disseminating—" The first man says as the second helps her out of her chair.

"Knitting patterns?" Mama is angry now. Her voice thunders through the house in a way Abby has never heard before. "This is absolutely ridiculous. We've done everything we were told. We got rid of the radio, for God's sake! Do you know how quiet it is without a radio?"

Abby can't help herself. "Mama!" she calls out, racing from her hiding place

Mama's eyes close tightly for just a moment, another gesture Abby knows well. Her mother is afraid, but she has trained herself too well to let it show. *Bella figura.* She is disciplined. She does not show her fear. Abby stops. She wants to run to her mother, to comfort and protect her the way her mother has always done for her, but she cannot move. If her mother is afraid, something terrible must be about to happen.

She smiles at Abby and whispers. Somehow Abby manages to hear. "Be good for your grandmother."

But there is no calming her.

Chapter Twenty-One

THAT NIGHT, ABBY SAT IN the food tent watching yet another sideshow versus ride jockeys euchre match. While the tent was drier than the last time, it was much colder inside. The temperature had dropped to about forty degrees, and Abby had wrapped herself in a wool blanket as she peered over Suprema's shoulder and examined her cards. "Play that one," she hissed.

Suprema laughed. "I can't. Ruth played a heart."

"Sorry, I'm not really good at this game," Ruth said somewhat sheepishly. "I play Jass."

"You're better than Abby," Suprema teased. "She just told me to play a—"

"No table talk!" shouted Jimmy, the ride jockey who ran the haunted train. He still wore his top hat and reminded Abby of Roman, but she didn't want to think about Roman. It made her think about Natale and Nonna and how her family was faring. She squeezed Suprema's hand, and Suprema smiled back at her. Abby had made the right decision, but that didn't mean it was always easy.

"Abby!" a voice called from the entrance to the tent. The entire group turned to look as Thomas hurried over to them. Della trailed behind, with her arms crossed and her face, still covered in cold cream, locked into a scowl. "I've been looking for you everywhere," he said.

"I—"

"He came to me first," Della practically spat. "Apparently little Tommy here is oblivious to the fact that you haven't been my trailer freeloader for two jumps!"

Abby didn't know what to say. Clearly Thomas didn't either. He looked at Della as if to say, "please don't hurt me," then held out an envelope to Abby, who snatched it. Della was still rambling on, about how she had to follow him and make sure the letter was hand-delivered because she wasn't about to be accused of withholding mail again. All Abby could do was give Thomas an apologetic shrug.

The envelope had no return address. At first, Abby thought the letter had come from Aunt Teresa. Her last letter had come without a return address. It surprised her that her aunt would reach out.

"Are we gonna finish this round?" Jimmy asked irritably. He pointed at the ace of clubs in the center of the table. "I just put down a trump, you see that there."

Suprema glared at him. "Could you, maybe—"

"It's okay," Abby said, kissing Suprema on the cheek. "I'll go read this. You play cards."

She slipped away to the edge of the tent and peeled back the flap of the envelope. The paper wasn't Aunt Teresa's pink and perfumed stationery. The envelope contained a novelty card. It was heart-shaped, and printed inside the heart was a flying saucer containing two cherubs and the words, "You're out of this world." Abby felt strange, as if she had forgotten something important. She held her breath and opened the card.

Abby,

I think I have been very patient allowing you to live out this little summer adventure you seemed so intent on, but now it is time for you to come home. I have booked passage on a train south to Urbana. I will meet the carnival there and collect you.

I know you may be resistant to this. A friend of mine who has been working with the carnival company has told me about your strange romance. My advice is to end this, and soon. It will only cause trouble for you down the road. And trouble for her. And, of course, for poor Natale, who has been doing his very best, but is certainly not innocent in all of this.

My friend has already seen to it that rumors will dog the carnival and that they will get worse if you do not come home with me.

I am eager to see you, Abby. I have missed you, but I have also been busy getting things ready for your return. I really think you will love the venue and I have already selected your favorite roses. By the way, did you enjoy the earrings? I never heard. I think that pearls suit you more than you might think. You should wear them to the wedding. They will look lovely with your dress.

Please be ready for me when I arrive. I would hate to see anything bad happen if you are not.

Your devoted,
FB

Abby stood staring at the words. She was barely able to breathe for fear that taking a breath after reading them meant that they were real. If it hadn't been for Della pulling the letter from her hand, she might have stood there holding it and staring at the words until Frank himself showed up to cart her away.

"This guy is royally screwy, Abby," Della said, not even thinking twice about scanning the letter's contents.

Still numb, Abby nodded.

"He can't hurt Natale. We can't let him."

This was the first thing Della had said that Abby agreed with in quite some time. "I know," she said, her heart aching. She glanced toward the euchre game. Suprema had just set down her card, and it must have been a good one because her face was adorned with a proud smirk. Abby's heart broke just thinking about what she needed to do. It wasn't just Natale that Frank was threatening. It was Suprema. It was the carnival as a whole. She turned away from the game and hung her head. "Don't worry. I'll go," she whispered.

"Like hell you will," Della spat. Her voice wasn't loud, but her words were vehement.

This startled Abby, who stared back at Della.

"We'll handle this Frank character. He won't know what hit him."

"I… I don't—" She glanced once more at the euchre game. Of all the people involved in the carnival, Della was the last one she could imagine being supportive. Ruth, definitely. Vinnie, probably. But Della? She hadn't seemed all that eager to get involved, even on the first night.

"Look, I have to tell you something." She scanned the tent and lowered her voice as if she were about to divulge the greatest secret of her life. Abby waited for something along the lines of "I am from outer space." Instead, Della blurted, "My mother didn't die in a trapeze accident." She stopped, looking at Abby, perhaps hoping to see what impact that made. When Abby continued to stare blankly, she barreled on. "My mother didn't die in a trapeze accident. She got married, had a baby, and left the circus. I always figured she might as well have died. That's what I always thought. Love steals your glory. What's the point of it? That's why I ran away, you know."

All Abby could do was nod. She had no idea what to make of Della's words.

"But I dunno. I've been thinking a lot and, I dunno. I mean." She stopped, frowning to herself as though the words refused to work their way out of her mouth. She touched a hand to her navel and took a deep breath. "I'm mad about your brother, Abby. Always have been.

Since the day I first saw him. Why do you think I kept that letter? I just wanted his handwriting near me, which is ridiculous, but—"

"I knew that," Abby said, surprising herself. Somehow, despite everything, it was the only explanation that made sense.

"No, you didn't." Della's eyes flashed, and Abby supposed it was best not to argue with her. "Look. I… I love him."

The pair stared at each other, sizing up the situation, and then Abby let her gaze drift over Della's shoulder and back to the euchre game. Suprema was laughing, a real and true laugh. It wasn't muffled or covered. She wasn't trying to stop herself. She was just letting the unfiltered joy of emotion escape, and it made Abby's pulse race. "It's not just Natale he said he'll hurt," she whispered, reaching out to take the card back from Della. "I can't—she doesn't deserve—"

"You're right. She deserves someone who's willing to fight for her."

Her words stung, but as Abby watched the girl she loved laugh and smile, she couldn't see any other way out. "I'm not some romantic heroine, Della. Girls like me aren't heroines."

"Not with that attitude, you're not."

Abby looked back into Della's eyes, leveling a glare that she hoped would rival Della's own, but she saw sincerity. "All right, then. What do you propose we do?"

"Well, we don't have a lot of time. I suppose—" She too turned around and examined the players. "I wonder if it would make any difference if we found out who this mole is. He's probably the one who told the police in Chicago that we were harboring 'secret communists,' as if there was such a thing!"

The thought made Abby feel sick. She had come to love and care for all of these people; could one of them really be a friend of Frank's? She refused to believe it. "He's probably bluffing. He bluffs. He always bluffs."

"Does he?" Della asked skeptically. "You seemed pretty sure he wasn't bluffing in July."

She rolled the card in her hand, trying to draw the nervousness from her mind. It didn't work. "I'm going to go."

"But we haven't thought of a plan."

"Later."

Abby walked to the table and peered down at the cards. Both teams only had one point left to go.

"You all right?" Suprema asked. Abby slipped her arm through hers and held on, perhaps a little tighter than she meant to. "Abby . . . ?"

She didn't know how to answer or explain. She simply held on to Suprema's arm. After a moment Suprema seemed to understand. She set her cards down and gently rubbed Abby's arm with her free hand.

"Don't worry, Suprema," Ruth said, putting on what seemed to Abby to be false confidence. "I've got a loner hand."

"You do not," Jimmy said.

Ruth narrowed her eyes and shook her head. "I'm going alone either way."

Jimmy looked put out, but Suprema nodded gratefully. She led Abby out of the tent. "Abby, what is it?"

"I'll tell you, I promise, but right now, can you just hold me?"

Suprema pulled her close, wrapped her arms around Abby, and gently stroked her hair. Abby breathed her in. She smelled sweet, like kettle corn, and the scent calmed Abby's racing mind. She turned her head up toward Suprema's face and kissed her gently as she slipped the card into her hand.

The kiss continued. Neither of them seemed willing to break it for quite some time. Abby's entire body cleared of the tension she had felt so intensely. She felt free and strong. Suprema's body and lips were warm, and the autumn chill that had been irritating her bones also seemed to disappear. She wanted to hold on to that feeling forever.

Too soon, Suprema pulled back and looked at the card. "Is this what Thomas brought you?"

Abby nodded slowly. She touched her fingertips to her chest, trying to hold on to the feeling she'd had while kissing Suprema.

"FB is—?"

"Yes." Oh, how she wanted none of this to be happening. She wanted that more than anything in the world.

"Oh, Abby … I'm so sorry."

"It's not your fault."

"I know. I just … I thought this was over."

"So did I. I'd almost forgotten him entirely."

"What are you going to do?"

Abby looked at the ground. Her mind started to run away with her again. "I don't know. I don't want go—"

"I don't want you to go," Suprema jumped in. Her face turned ashen.

They both breathed deeply, watching one another. Before either of them realized what was happening, they were kissing once again, with the fierce passion of two people who have suddenly had their time together cut short. They each held on tight, as though terrified the other would disappear if they dared slacken their grip in the slightest. Abby figured she could come up with a plan later, when the world around her didn't feel quite so urgent.

Chapter Twenty-Two

THE NEXT FEW DAYS IN Urbana were tense. Abby wanted, more than anything, to enjoy what little time she had left with Suprema, but she was a bundle of nerves and found calming herself difficult. Suprema tried, and Abby tried to reassure her that her gentle kisses and the careful but strong way that she held her did help, but her mind wouldn't still. She was too afraid. She hoped, deep down, that Suprema knew this wasn't a reflection of her feelings for her.

She spent most of the week trying to concoct a plan that had even the remotest chance of success. She even fell asleep one night while combing through a mental list of places she might be able to convince Suprema to run away to.

Her bally was also weak; her voice faltered as she scanned the crowds for Frank's face. Whereas once she had seen it everywhere, now he seemed to be lurking just out of sight, just behind the curtain of the tent across the midway, or hidden from view by the crowds shuffling by. She never saw him, but she felt his presence everywhere.

At the end of her latest attempt at "The Flying Saucer Blues," a high-pitched voice that seemed out of place jolted her from her thoughts. "Aaabbbyyy!" the voice called out from down the midway. Annette had rushed onto the platform and was clinging to her leg before Abby fully understood what was happening.

"Annette?" she asked breathlessly, not daring to believe it.

"Are there really aliens in there?" Annette asked, looking up at her wide-eyed and hopeful.

"Annette, where did you come from?"

Natale's voice jarred her even more. "Cleveland, which is four hours from here, by the way. You could have mentioned that in your letter. You know, before I put four small children in a car with me. I don't have a radio, Abby."

Abby laughed. It was the first time she had laughed in days. She rushed down the bally platform and gathered as many of her siblings into a hug as her arms would contain.

"Yeah, yeah, we're happy to see you, too," Leon said, squirming.

"You came?" She almost couldn't believe it.

Natale shrugged. "You were right. The kids needed a break. And Geauga Lake is played out."

"Wow, I rank higher than the Big Dipper?"

Leon raised an eyebrow. "Are you telling me that we—"

"No," Natale said.

"We have a roller coaster," Abby said, smirking at Leon's sulk. "But first, who wants to see aliens?"

Joseph raised a tentative hand. Carla nodded and Annette squealed. "I suppose," said Leon.

"Right this way, then!" Abby led them into the tent. As she did so, Natale caught her by the wrist.

"Can you keep an eye on them for a bit?" he asked in a hushed tone.

"Natale, I'm working," Abby hissed.

"Just for a little while. I have to find Della. We need to talk."

Abby glanced at the four youngest Amaros oohing and ahhing over several jars of green sludge. "Fine."

"They haven't eaten yet, so—"

"Don't push it, Natale."

He doffed his hat almost mockingly before ducking away. Abby shook her head and went back to watching her younger siblings. She hoped that Natale and Della would reconcile, especially considering how desperate Della had been the other night. She wanted them to be happy, after all.

An hour later, when Natale hadn't returned and Leon had begun whining that he was "really booored," she closed up the attraction and started down the midway.

"Can we play a game?" Carla asked timidly.

"Or go on the haunted train?" cried an excited Annette.

"Maybe later. I need to find Natale, or anyone else to help me wrangle you four." She looked into each booth, hoping to spot Ruth or Boleslaw, even Vinnie, someone better with kids to keep them distracted.

"Natale went to look for the—" Annette began, but stopped when Joseph shushed her.

"Look for the what?" Abby asked, as a twinge of fear prickled her spine. Did he not tell her the whole story of why they came? Was Frank here? Was he going to confront Frank? And why would he bring the little ones if that were his plan?

"I'm hungry," Annette whined.

"Me too," Joseph whispered.

Abby sighed and glanced at Carla and Leon, who both shrugged. "If you know anything, you should tell me."

As one, all four shook their heads.

Crossing her arms, Abby narrowed her eyes at them. She couldn't go looking for Natale with them in tow, though. "Let's get you something to eat."

Verboten as it was, Abby led the crew to the food tent. If she were going to find anyone to help her, it would be there. She started toward the sideshow folks, who had sequestered themselves in the far corner.

"I think we've finally convinced my mother to come to Florida for the winter," Ruth was saying as they approached. "What was holding her to New Philadelphia, I cannot possibly—" she broke off as Abby approached. "The young Amaros, I assume?"

Annette bowed. The entire group laughed, and the little girl's face broke into a broad grin.

"Have you seen Suprema?" Abby asked, glancing around the group and not finding her face.

"She went to get you," Constance offered. "She should be back soon."

"Is that snake real?" Carla asked of Gregor, who still had his python draped over his shoulders.

Gregor nodded. "Her name is Lucy; want to hold her?"

Abby stopped herself from interceding when Carla nodded enthusiastically. The other three backed away, terror-stricken.

"Hold out your arms," Gregor said. Carla obeyed, and he gently set Lucy across them. Abby was relieved to see that the snake remained uncoiled. After a tense moment, Carla laughed.

"Me next!" Leon said, regaining his composure.

"Of course, and then I need to speak with your sister."

This made Abby uneasy, and she was grateful that moments later Suprema appeared in the tent. "Sorry, I forgot about lunch," Abby said as Suprema slipped up beside her. "Look who showed up."

Suprema smiled to see Abby's brothers and sisters, but with a hint of worry.

"Is something wrong?" Abby asked.

"Gregor and I were talking," she said, now watching as Constance showed Annette and Joseph how to pass their hands through a flame without being burned. To Abby's relief, neither looked willing to try it. "We were trying to come up with a plan and—"

"I want to… to make it up to you," Gregor whispered in a voice so low Abby barely heard it. She wasn't entirely sure that she hadn't made up the words.

"Excuse me?"

"I want to make it up to you," he repeated, just a little louder, lifting Lucy from Leon's arms and looking toward Abby with a determined expression.

"What do you mean?"

Suprema squeezed her hand. "Do you think, if Gregor challenged Frank to a fair rematch because he had been humiliated before, that Frank would be able to resist it?"

"I don't know," Abby said. She didn't like this idea. Frank didn't like to get into situations where he didn't know he could win, but underneath all the calculation was a great deal of pride. Frank was unpredictable when his pride was challenged. For starters, she'd never thought he'd follow her. She had been certain he would give up. If he felt challenged, would he fight? "He's probably pretty certain he's better than you. He's probably convinced himself of that, anyway."

"I wanted to do it, but he sounds like the kind of guy who would get all chivalric about fighting a girl," Suprema said.

Abby was about to contradict this by saying that he'd fought a girl before, but she shook her head. "I don't know that it would help."

Suprema slipped her arm around Abby's waist and whispered, "Let me try to protect you."

"No," Abby whispered in return. She didn't like it. There were too many things that could go wrong. "This is my battle."

"Abby …"

Abby looked at Suprema and tried to say with her eyes what she couldn't say with her voice: "I love you. I've seen him hurt too many people. I can't let him hurt you." Suprema looked back at her. Though her eyes seemed to say she understood, there also didn't seem to be any moving her. "I need to think about it," she said.

"From what Suprema told me, we don't know how much time we have," Gregor began.

"Time for what?" Della asked, coming up to the group. Natale's coat was draped around her shoulders, and their hands were interlaced.

Natale's eyes were trained on Della. He didn't even notice Gregor. They looked like many a couple Abby had seen at the diner, and despite everything it made her smile.

"Did you find the baby?" Annette asked, very businesslike.

Della's eyes flew open. "You told them?!"

"No," Natale said. "What are you talking about, Annette?"

"Joseph and I found your letter."

"And you read it?"

"Yes." Her lack of shame sent a giggle through the sideshow performers.

"It's not funny," Della protested.

Abby shook her head. She would let Natale deal with Annette and Joseph's transgressions. "Is that what had you so… upset?" she asked of Della.

Della smiled. "I had a lot of thinking to do about what I wanted, that's all. I had expected our conversation to go much differently, and well…"

"I don't mind if she keeps up the aerial act," Natale said, lifting Della's hand to his lips. "Maybe with some precautions—"

"No triples," Della said with a roll of her eyes.

"This calls for a celebration, yes?" Ruth said. Della and Natale nodded, beaming at each other, and Abby was glad for the shift in attention, away from her.

"Is the haunted train a celebration?" Annette asked.

"I don't know if we should reward her," Natale began.

"Pleeeaase?"

"Oh, come on, Natale," Abby said, glancing at Suprema with a sly smile. She wouldn't mind going on the ride with her. Suprema's nose was wrinkled, and she did not look quite as pleased to have the subject changed as Abby was, but after a moment she nodded indulgently.

Chapter Twenty-Three

The group set off as one. Abby felt a strange sensation grip her. A small voice at the back of her mind was telling her to take it all in, because she might not have another chance. She examined the caravan around her. Just two months ago, she didn't know any of these people. Now, she recognized them. She knew that the woman unfurling the flags that read "French Fries!" and "Funnel Cakes!" was named Mimi, and she had three children to support. It was strange how much had changed.

They paced through the midway, past the games and rides and vendors, until they reached the haunted train. The trailer had been uncovered, and the cars had been detached. They sat on the grass in front. A sign with a painted ghost also lay in the dirt nearby. Abby felt a gnawing deep in her stomach. "Back again?" Jimmy teased.

"What's going on, Jimmy?" Ruth asked, reaching out toward him with genuine concern. "Are you in some sort of trouble?"

"I had a long night."

"Why's it torn down?" Annette asked in a plaintive voice, as though someone had just told her there was no such thing as unicorns.

Abby felt ill when she looked at Jimmy. He looked the same as ever, top hat and all, but for the first time, she didn't see the resemblance to Sal or Roman. She saw Frank. "No. Not you. Anyone but you." The whole group looked at Abby. Most of them looked confused, but on the faces of Suprema and Della, understanding dawned.

Behind her, a familiar voice spoke. "Hey, Abby."

She froze. She knew that voice, and had never wanted to hear that voice again. She didn't turn to look at him. She didn't have to. She knew exactly what he looked like, standing there in the middle of the midway. He would look out of place: too-nice slacks, paired with a too-new leather jacket and hat, like someone trying too hard to cut an imposing figure. His brown hair would be swept into a ducktail in his best effort to look like James Dean, but it would only serve to further the impression that he was trying too hard. His shoes would be freshly polished, but now a little scuffed thanks to the dusty midway. He wouldn't be happy with that. And if he wasn't flanked by a few friends or flunkies, they would be nearby.

"Go away, Frank," she said, still not turning.

"You all ready to go?"

"What the hell are you doing here?" Natale snarled. Della rested her arm on his. He didn't move any closer to Frank, but still clenched his fist.

"Abby invited me."

"I most certainly did not."

"We know, Abby," Suprema whispered.

Frank grinned like a comic book villain. "Look who's here! We've got to get you to safety, lickety split, Abs. That crazy strongwoman and her buddy Gregory could snap you in half. You need someone like me to protect you."

"You know that was stupid the first time you said it, right?" Abby said with a roll of her eyes.

Frank stared; his eyes bored into her. "You're really going to talk to me like that? That is, certainly, not an appropriate tone of voice for my wife to take with me."

"I'm not your wife. You are delusional."

"These carnies have ruined you. What happened to your manners?"

Abby flinched. Every nerve in her body was firing, fast and furious. Frank's tone was too familiar. She knew exactly what was about to happen and squeezed her eyes shut, bracing for it.

It never came. When she opened her eyes, Frank had stumbled to the ground and was rubbing at his eye. "I thought you were supposed to fight by the rules," he growled.

"Like you did?" Suprema asked, a confident smirk dancing across her face. She wrapped her arm around Abby's waist, and Abby felt her nerves relax one by one. She was safe and loved.

"This is pointless; we don't have to fight." He stood again, still holding his hand over his eye.

"Yeah, Suprema, this doesn't need to involve us," Jimmy added, stepping out from his ticket booth and entering the fray. "I mean, unless you *want* your uncle branded a communist."

"Jimmy ..." There was a warning note in her voice that could not be ignored. He was, as far as Suprema was concerned, one of them; she didn't want to have to fight him, but Abby could tell that she would if she had to.

Abby shook her head. "Suprema, don't," she said quietly. "There's a way to resolve this without anyone getting hurt." She didn't want a fight, not in front of her siblings.

Suprema sighed, sounding disappointed but resigned. "I'm sure I can handle the two of them." Abby had no doubt that she could. They stood, not moving, staring her down, and Abby could see the fear in Jimmy's eyes, despite his clear effort to hide it. He didn't want to have to fight either.

"And besides, you're outnumbered!" Natale called.

"Yeah!" Leon added.

"Oh yes, I can see that," Frank mused. "But you either back down or my insurance takes care of it."

"I don't care about your insurance or whatever you're up to," Suprema said, cutting him off. She looked at Abby; her face was soft, reassuring, full of love and faith. It made Abby feel strong. "He's not coming anywhere near you. Not ever again."

Chapter Twenty-Four

SHOUTS OF "HEY, RUBE!" ECHOED throughout the carnival. Every soul who had ever had their monthly pay come from Mr. or Mrs. McClure came running when they heard the call. Concessions and games closed. Rides stopped. The cavalry was on the way.

Frank was splayed on his back, struggling to get to his feet and screaming obscenities. Suprema stood over him with a fierce expression. "Don't you go anywhere near her."

"I'll do what I damn well please," Frank shouted, finally scrambling to his feet. As he did so, Jimmy ducked behind Suprema and grabbed Abby by the arm. She tried hard to pull away, but did not have the strength.

"Let her go," Suprema growled.

"Why would she want you? I mean, look at you!" Frank shouted, moving toward Suprema. He smirked, looking her over as if trying to appraise an antique. "You're some kind of mutant. Were you built in some Russian lab, like Frankenstein?"

"Frank, shut the hell up!" Abby screamed, trying hard to step on Jimmy's feet.

Frank lunged forward to grab Suprema by the arms, and that is when chaos erupted. The carnival workers moved forward to intervene. There were easily enough of them to overpower the two men. Frank smirked broadly. His confidence made Abby sick. She assumed it was only because he still somehow believed that he could take on the entire carnival. Then, he whistled. Was this the "insurance plan" Frank was rambling on about? A large group of people she had never seen before moved forward. Whether they were locals or hired thugs, Abby could not say. But before she knew what was happening, they were in the fray, and an all-out brawl had ensued.

"Suprema!" Abby called out, still trying to pull away from Jimmy. But he held tight, trying to make his way through the crowd and away from the fight.

"Abby! Where are you?" Della shouted from somewhere in the fray.

Abby swung her free arm as hard as she could, hitting Jimmy in the stomach. He shoved her away from him and that was all she needed. She ducked away, escaping into the crowd and disappearing.

"Abby!" a voice called from somewhere on the edge of the chaos. Then another. Abby moved toward the voices and saw that it was Ruth and Vivian. They had gathered Della and the younger Amaros. Leon kept trying to wrench away from Ruth, who was holding him back with a surprising show of strength.

"This way!" Vivian hissed, pressing her hand into the small of Abby's back and hurrying her along.

"What about Suprema? Natale?" Abby asked, frantically, looking back at the fight. The groups of carnies and locals all seemed to have blended into one mass. Abby couldn't see Suprema or Frank or Natale or Constance or anyone that she knew. "Where is she?"

"She'll be fine. She can handle herself," Vivian said snappishly. They hurried through the caravan which, for the first time since Abby had arrived, appeared to be completely deserted. Abby didn't want to think about what that meant.

"Come on," Vivian urged.

They all made their way to the Lambrinos's trailer, outside of which a frightened looking Phebe waited with Alejo, who was holding a vicious-looking knife.

“Are you all right?” Ruth asked. Her eyes were wild, full of a barely concealed panic as she rushed forward and clung to Phebe.

“I don’t know anything,” Vivian said, gently touching the top of Phebe’s head. “Let’s just all get inside.”

Alejo nodded, not saying a word. His eyes were directed toward the fight, where he knew as well as anyone that his daughter was in the fray.

“I can do more than blow smoke rings, Miss Amaro. No one’s coming anywhere near you.”

“It’s not me I’m worried about,” Abby whispered. Ruth squeezed her hand before they slipped inside.

Abby could hear her heart pounding in her ears. “I’m so sorry,” she whispered to Ruth, to herself, to no one in particular.

Ruth nodded. She stroked Phebe’s hair, perhaps to comfort herself as much as Phebe. “We protect our own,” she said. “No matter what anyone says. We. Protect. Our. Own.” There was a fierceness in her voice, and Abby knew that even though she was scared, she truly believed what she was saying. Over and over, the people of the carnival had reminded her that she was a part of their world. She finally, in that instant, believed it.

“That’s what I should be doing,” Abby said, glancing toward the window.

Annette was crying, which had distracted Leon enough to keep him from rushing to the fight. He was holding her so close, it broke Abby’s heart. She remembered him holding baby Annette at their mother’s funeral and hoped that they wouldn’t have to experience another for a long time.

Della wasn’t speaking. She stared numbly at the wall, holding both Carla’s and Joseph’s hands. Neither of them had let go, but from the way that they both kept nervously looking at her face, she was definitely crushing their fingers.

“Help me make cocoa. It’ll keep your mind busy,” Ruth said, finally letting go of Phebe.

"It's not that. I mean, sure, I'd fight if I could, but it's not that..."

Ruth watched her. Her eyes held none of Constance's ever-present patience, but it was clear that she was trying to replicate the expression for Abby's sake.

"I'm not one of you, Ruth. I'm just a girl who went on an adventure, and now it's time to go home before anyone gets hurt or goes to jail."

"With all due respect, that is absolutely absurd." All attempts at faked patience had vanished from Ruth's eyes. "I didn't think I fit in here at first either," she began. "Carnies, they're distrustful of outsiders. It comes with the trade. Abby, you can deny it all you want, but you're part of the troupe now. And this troupe has your back. Do you think that many people would have come to your aid otherwise?"

"I still don't—" She stopped speaking when Phebe climbed into her lap.

"I'd have your back if I were allowed," she said in a calm and determined voice.

Abby had to grin. "Well, I know which of your *madres* you get that tone of voice from."

"Oh, I don't know about that," Ruth began, but before she could finish, they heard a loud thwack not far from the trailer.

"Don't come any closer," Alejo said just outside the door. "That was on purpose."

Abby and Ruth both looked at each other with wide eyes and nodded. Without exchanging words, Abby gave Phebe to Ruth and slipped toward the door.

"I just want to talk to Abby," Frank said, arms outstretched, looking pleadingly at Alejo. His leather jacket was torn, his hair was disheveled, and a small bruise under his eye was beginning to darken.

"How did he get away?" Abby hissed. "I swear, if he hurt her, or anyone else for that matter—"

"Abby!" he called out, catching sight of her.

"Stay behind me," Alejo cautioned.

"No." Abby moved around Alejo and took a few steps toward Frank. "Why are you doing this? Is—am I … really worth all this?"

"Abby …" Frank tone was apologetic. She'd heard it before. He always knew when he'd gone too far, but this time, this time was much, much too far. There was no coming back from it.

"No, Frank. This is too much, and I think you know it too."

He stared at her, not speaking or even blinking. She knew that he was still capable of causing plenty of harm to the people she loved and cared about. He could hurt her family. He could spread rumors about Suprema and Boleslaw. He could hurt or even kill her. She knew all of that, but she didn't know how else to end it. She wasn't a fighter. She didn't have strength behind her fist. She couldn't throw knives or pass her hand through fire without feeling the pain. This last-ditch effort was the best she had, and the only thing she knew how to do.

"I'm staying with the carnival, Frank. This is what I need to do for me to be happy, and I love Suprema … and I don't love you."

She saw fury flash in Frank's eyes, but then, miraculously, she saw it waver and fade into doubt. "But—"

Countless moments flashed before her. The dance, when he had pushed her for dancing with another boy. The lakeshore, when he tried to explain that he was going to mess around with other girls, but that didn't mean she couldn't be his girlfriend because who else would want her, after all? The diner, when he wouldn't take no for an answer. Clear, now, she shook her head. "No, Frank. No. For once in your life, for once in our entire time knowing one another, can you respect my decision?"

Frank was quiet, quieter than Abby had ever seen him. He seemed to be completely out of witty, proud retorts and sarcastic comments. He stared hard for a long time, but Abby did not look away. She met his eyes, stared into their hazel fog, and he stared back into hers. They would never understand one another, but she tried. With her eyes, she tried to say exactly what she had said with words. That she loved Suprema. That she needed to stay. In that instant, Frank's eyes changed. She could have sworn she saw the shift take place, and that she witnessed the second he let go.

He nodded. "I maintain that you've made a mistake, but, you know what, you're right. Plenty of fish in the sea. Plenty of better fish than you."

He turned and was gone. Abby couldn't find it in her heart to be offended.

~July, 1956~

ABBY LOOKS OUT ACROSS THE lake and tries to pretend that it's the ocean. The lake itself is vast, and it doesn't take much imagination to achieve her goal. She focuses hard on the waves lapping at the horizon. If she didn't know better, she'd say that the water went on forever.

"Look at me! I'm a mermaid!" Carla shouts, splashing both legs in the water at the same time.

"Me too!" Annette cries, doing the same.

"Careful, you two," Abby says with a smile. "You don't want to get too far in."

"We're mermaids. It doesn't matter how far in we go," Annette says matter-of-factly, and Abby has to laugh. She can't stop herself.

Back on the grass, Natale has finished setting up the picnic and is trying to corral Leon and Joseph away from their stick-based swordfight and back to the table. Nonna sits and watches this exchange with an amused expression.

"Lunch is ready, girls," Abby says, handing towels to both of them and leading them back to the spread of antipasti and sandwiches. Nonna helps prepare the plates when they finally all convene. The six of them wait before digging in as Nonna crosses herself and says a silent prayer.

"What do you pray for, Nonna?" Joseph asks.

Both Abby and Natale's eyes widen as they shush him.

Nonna just smiles. "That someday, all of my grandchildren will be happy and smiling and that all of their dreams will come true, even if it is in ways that they do not expect."

The summer air is warm even this close to the lake, and Abby smiles, trying to hold on to the happiness of this moment for rest of her life.

Epilogue

~Late July, 1958. Cleveland, Ohio fairgrounds.~

The banner strung between two poles near the brand-new, above-ground swimming pool read, "Real! Singing Sirens! Alive!" with two dark-haired cartoon mermaids, one with a red tail, the other with a blue one, painted on either side of the words. Abby liked the sign, though she hadn't expected to. She didn't exactly have top billing. Her name wasn't anywhere on it. In fact, her name wasn't anywhere associated with the show. Still, something in those three exclamation points, which proclaimed to all the world that she was a real, living being, put a huge grin on her face.

"Did you see the new sign?" Ruth asked as Abby slipped into the dressing tent. She was already dressed in her navy bathing suit, which was styled after Esther Williams's and grinning from ear to ear. It looked as though she had tried to tame her curls, but had given up, letting them fly about. Abby had assured her numerous times that this looked more appropriate for the mermaids they were playing.

"I like it," Abby answered, sitting down at the vanity to touch up her supposedly waterproof makeup. "They almost look like us."

"Well, that might be a little bit of a stretch, but I do think it's very nice."

"Knock, knock," Constance's voice called from outside.

"We're decent!" Abby called back.

"Pity," Suprema said, as she pulled back the canvas and she and Constance came inside.

Abby laughed. They embraced briefly before Abby pulled back, beaming. "Did you see the sign? I'm on a sign!"

Suprema and Constance exchanged amused expressions, and then nodded. "Our little girls, all grown up and getting their own sign!" the two of them teased in one voice. It was clear that they had rehearsed this line, knowing that either Abby or Ruth or both would gush about the new sign.

Ruth and Abby shook their heads. They had been expecting such a reaction. Ruth took her sequined tail out of its case. "You should hurry up, Abby," she said. "We're on in ten minutes." Then she linked her arm through Constance's and the pair disappeared from the tent.

Nodding, Abby took a long deep breath. She hadn't been nervous about the act until just now. She knew the routine inside and out. She and Ruth had been practicing for months. Still, an old, unnamed terror gripped her stomach.

Suprema touched her arm. "Don't be nervous," she whispered.

"Nervous," Abby said, trying to make the word sound ridiculous and failing. "When did I ever say I was nervous? Why would I be nervous?"

"It's written all over every inch of you."

Abby didn't have any answer for that. Instead, she closed her eyes and held tight to Suprema, breathing in the kettle-corn smell of her.

"I'll be out there, cheering you on. We all will," Suprema said, stroking her hair. "But you don't need it. You're going to be the biggest hit we've had in years."

Abby couldn't help the blush that developed at those words, but she didn't try to hide it. She turned to look up into Suprema's eyes. They held each other's gaze for a just a moment before she stood on her tiptoes and reached up for a kiss.

"Sing 'Mambo Italiano,'" a voice called out from the audience as the singing sirens finished their rendition of "Beyond the Sea."

"No, no! 'Baciami'!" called another.

Ruth raised an eyebrow. "I assume you know them?" She moved her feet a little, flicking the fake tail so that water splashed out. Not enough to hit anyone in the crowd, but enough to make them laugh and gasp.

Abby glanced at the crowd and, sure enough, saw Sal and Roman squeezed into the front row with Natale and the rest of her siblings and her father. She beamed at all of them, and they broke into thunderous applause for her. She was still shocked to see her father out and about. Natale had reported that since Christmas, when the whole family made the trek to Nashville by train, he'd been appearing in public more and more, but it remained hard for Abby to believe.

"I don't think I know those songs," she said, feigning innocence and confusion. "But I do have one I think that you'll love."

Behind the pool, Vinnie began to play his accordion. Abby breathed deeply, allowing her eyes to linger on each one of her family members: Annette, squirming at the very edge of the row; Carla, currently sharing her chair with Phebe; Joseph, kicking his feet in anticipation; Leon, whose arms were crossed as though he didn't want to be at something so childish, but whose smiling eyes gave him away; her father, wide awake, smiling, and aware; and finally Della, who rested her head on Natale's shoulder. The pair of them smiled as well. Della raised her hand to show off the small ring on her finger, and Abby couldn't help herself. She laughed. Natale did as well, his eyes alight. Abby's heart surged with happiness for him, and she hoped his did for her as well. She only knew one way to say it. She began to sing the folk song that had changed her life, and before she knew it, all of them were singing along.

This time, just after sunset, was still Abby's favorite part of the day. The lights of the carnival midway were just beginning to flicker to life, shrouding the already entertaining world in a glow of mystery and enchantment. The carnival wasn't a cocoon as the diner had been. People could still get hurt by the carnival. A heart could still break at the carnival. Yet no matter how hard she had once fought it, her heart was here. Looking out over the crowd, she could see, in the very back, that same astonishing, pretty, chiseled face that she had seen her first night. In the arms of the strongwoman in the leopard-print suit—that was where she could truly find herself, safe.

Acknowledgments

First and foremost, I need to thank my family. It would take far too long to thank each of them individually as I have been blessed with a very large, diverse, and supportive extended family, but thank you all. Thank you for being open with me about your lives and your hearts. Thank you for indulging and supporting my dream of being a storyteller and never wavering in your faith in me. Every one of you means more to me than you can possibly imagine or even vaguely realize.

To the team at Interlude Press for getting this book out to the world and for your commitment to seeing the diversification of literature in general.

To Mark, who patiently reads my drafts, talks me through my frustrations, and keeps me grounded.

To Rachel, who has known me longer than anyone outside my family and because this really is all your fault. I hope you know that.

To Elizabeth, my lovely beta reader, thank you for all your constructive (and highly witty) feedback. Every writer needs someone like you to fall back on.

And, of course, this book would be nowhere without the amazing archivists, librarians, authors, historians, and museum curators who helped facilitate my research and writing and who helped me take recollections and expand them into a reality, and to explore a world and time that I had never known. I would especially like to thank the Western Reserve Historical Society for their collections of Italian-American and LGBT historical materials, both of which were immensely helpful in my research, as well as the following invaluable authors for their books: *Secrets of Sideshows* by Joe Nickell; *My Life with Geeks, Freaks, & Vagabonds in the Carny Trade*, the autobiography of Howard Bone; and *A Pictorial History of the American Carnival* by Joe McKennon.

About the Author

Amy Stilgenbauer is a writer and archivist currently based in southeast Michigan. She is the author of the young adult novel, *The Legend of League Park*, and her short story, "The Fire-Eater's Daughter," was included in *Summer Love: An LGBTQ Collection* published by Duet, the young adult imprint of Interlude Press. When not working, she stays busy gardening, playing trivia, and keeping her cats away from her knitting.

One **story**
can change **everything.**

@interlude**press**

Twitter | Facebook | Instagram | Pinterest | Tumblr

For a reader's guide to ***Sideshow*** *and book club prompts, please visit interludepress.com.*

also from amy **stilgenbauer**

"The Fire-Eater's Daughter"
Summer Love: An LGBTQ Collection

When a traveling carnival comes back to town, Ruth must choose between caring for her mother and a life with the beautiful and mysterious Constance, the fire-eater's daughter. The Fire-Eater's Daughter is a short story originally published in *Summer Love*, an LGBTQ young adult collection published by Duet, an imprint of Interlude Press.

Summer Love : An LGBTQ Collection **ISBN (print) 978-1-941530-59-7 | (eBook) 978-1-941530-60-3**

Short Story ISBN (eBook) 978-1-941530-90-0

interlude press™
now available…

Burning Tracks by Lilah Suzanne

In the sequel to *Broken Records*, Gwen Pasternak has it all: a job she loves as a celebrity stylist and a beautiful wife, Flora. But as her excitement in working with country music superstar Clementine Campbell grows, Gwen second-guesses her quiet domestic bliss. Meanwhile, her business partner, Nico Takahashi and his partner, reformed bad-boy musician Grady Dawson, face uncertainties of their own.

ISBN (print) 978-1-941530-99-3 | (eBook) 978-1-945053-00-9

Speakeasy by Suzey Ingold

In the height of the Prohibition era in Manhattan, recent Yale graduate Heath Johnson falls for Art, the proprietor of a unique speakeasy where men are free to explore their sexuality. When Art's sanctuary is raided, Heath is forced to choose between love and the structured life his parents planned for him.

ISBN (print) 978-1-941530-69-6 | (eBook) 978-1-941530-70-2

Right Here Waiting by K.E. Belledonne

In 1942, Ben Williams had it all—a fulfilling job, adoring friends and the love of his life, Pete Montgomery. But World War II looms over them. When Pete follows his conscience and joins the Army Air Force as a bomber pilot, Ben must find the strength to stay behind without his lover, the dedication to stay true and the courage he never knew he'd need to discover his own place in the war effort.

ISBN (print) 978-1-941530-22-1 | (eBook) 978-1-941530-28-3

www.ingramcontent.com/pod-product-compliance
Lightning Source LLC
LaVergne TN
LVHW091140080826
845145LV00008B/2208

* 9 7 8 1 9 4 5 0 5 3 0 1 6 *